DEATH IN COLD WATERS

A gripping psychological suspense murder
mystery

Tannis Laidlaw

Forth Estate Books

Forth Estate Books :tannis@tannislaidlaw.com

Publisher's Note: This is a work of fiction. Names, characters, and incidents are a product of the
author's imagination. Locales and public names are sometimes used for atmospheric purposes. Any
resemblance to actual people, living or dead, or to businesses, events, institutions, or locales is
completely coincidental.

Death in Cold Waters: ISBN 978-0-473-62418-7

"Man is not what he thinks he is; he is what he hides."

— André Malraux —

Chapter One

U nder the green canopy of low branches that filters the sunlight and ensures concealment, the body floats, sometimes bumping against the shore of the Thames before floating free again. Only a few metres up the slope, the towpath winds below a wide grassy embankment in front of houses in the distance; this side, bushes, trees and the occasional track lead down to the water's edge.

The only person who knows the body is in its green and wet bower runs easily along the towpath. He extends the distance with loping strides, exhilaration and fear jostling for dominance in his mind.

He knows the area well. As a child, playing in the bushes right on the river had been strictly forbidden but the riverbank had exerted its influence, drawing him like a magnet. Such a magical place to play – when little, with other boys his age, when a teenager fuelled by hormone-angst, watching young girls. This place was special.

With those thoughts, he reduces his speed as he jogs along the path. Slows as he passes more lush bushes leaning over the shoreline, memories of girls playing in the sunshine.

Better than thinking of the body lightly bumping the muddy shore of the Thames.

Better than thinking about Whatsername who would never go home again.

Chapter Two

The evening before, Madeleine Brooks stuffed the unfinished work into a plastic sleeve as she prepared to leave work.

"I see the reports are not in," Romania said from behind Maddie. "You know the rules. All reports in a full 24 hours before they're due. No exceptions. I shouldn't have to tell you that, Madeleine. You, of all people."

"We made that rule to give us plenty of time to go over the junior Service Officers' reports," Maddie said. "The directive wasn't meant for the senior staff." The irritation at being treated like an ignorant underling came to a slow boil inside her. This was not the first time.

Romania didn't deign to discuss the rule she had adapted. "Nine tomorrow. Don't be late."

Maddie jammed the folder into her business bag. Before leaving, she took off her I.D. 'Madeleine Brooks – Senior Probation Officer' and dropped the tag into her top drawer. Her position hadn't changed. Even if the work had.

• • • • •• • • • •

Maddie used her backside to push open the door of her house in Surbiton. Her hands were full: the business bag from work, her handbag and the groceries she'd bought on her way home.

"Anybody here?" she called.

Silence greeted her query. Not to worry; she could get dinner prepared before the impatient duo returned. She headed straight to the kitchen to dump everything on the table. Not before noticing that Wayne, in spite of fresh promises, had still not begun refurbishing the kitchen cabinet doors.

Chicken curry tonight. She liked to construct her curries from scratch. No factory packed curry powder for her. From her spices drawer she grabbed the vials of turmeric, cumin, fenugreek and chili pepper and the coriander from one of the supermarket bags and set to work. Soon zesty smells were filling her kitchen and she could pause. A chance to take her business bag up to her home office.

Once there, her irritation flooded back. Damn that woman. Throwing her considerable weight around. Differentially piling the report writing onto her shoulders. Never ending paperwork. Ordering her around as if she was the newcomer rather than her. Maddie dropped the files onto her desk without a care. Another hour's work at least. Her evening's entertainment. She went back downstairs to check on the burbling pot on the stove.

Maddie had always prided herself on doing a good job. A senior Probation Officer at Surrey and Sussex Probation Trust, long-term employee, who, when her beloved supervisor decided to retire and gave her the nod, had been confident she'd been chosen for promotion.

Not so.

They, whoever 'they' were, had decided new blood was needed. Change. And a replacement had been brought in from the north. Affirmative action, some of her colleagues had said with a sly grin. Their new supervisor, Romania Carlisle, was obviously, enthusiastically and belligerently gay. Sorry, LGBT. Or, to be pedantic, lgbtqqip2saa … the ever-expanding attempt to give everybody their own initial. Also, Romania was young.

Maddie was unexpectedly feeling her 49 years. Almost 50. At the height of her whatevers, she told herself. But no longer with a goal. And the extra money would have been nice.

The front door slammed.

"Who's home?" Maddie called.

"Your ever lovin'," Wayne called back. "Hungry as a…."

"Pig?"

He came into the kitchen, swiping at her bottom with his hand. "Talking about bears…"

"Were we?" She grinned at him. "You've been at the studio?"

"Jamming with Rick."

Rick, part of his group. They produced esoteric albums highly appreciated by a few, very few, diehard fans. Maddie's salary kept the mortgage paid and food on the table and, indeed, the rent paid for the studio space he shared with four other musicians. Not that she was complaining. She and Wayne had a twenty-six year marriage, longer than any of her close friends.

She heard a click. Must be her daughter sneaking in.

"Jade? Dinner in about fifteen minutes."

"Yeah, okay." Footsteps sluggishly sounded on the stairs.

She walked like Maddie felt. Slow. Enfeebled. Jade was seventeen.

"Did Butchy-Bitch load you up again with paperwork?" Wayne asked as he set the table in the kitchen. Since Olivia had left home to live with her then boyfriend, they'd stopped eating at the dining room table. Now they only used it when Olivia and her family were over for a meal. In a way, Maddie felt she was slacking. But it was difficult being formal when she was the only one comfortable with it. She glanced at Wayne. He was wearing cargo shorts he must have owned for at least a decade and they looked it. And a faded t-shirt advertising a Rolling Stones tour they did in 1978. Scuffed sandals. He dressed exactly the same way he'd dressed when they'd met in 1992. She'd bought him that vintage t-shirt off the internet a few years ago. It had become his favourite and still was. Now it looked as if it had actually been worn since 1978.

"Don't use that name," Maddie said as she saw Jade slip into the kitchen. She passed the full plates around. "I might be tempted to call her that in polite company." But she smiled to take any sting away.

"Did she?"

Maddie sighed. "Probably an hour's work tonight."

Soon after Romania had started, she'd decided that the Probation Service Officers, who were assigned the easier cases, weren't up to writing suitably concise reports for the courts. What she needed was an experienced Probation Officer to clean up the wordy and overly passionate reports produced by the Service Officers. Aha. She had just the person in Madeleine Brooks, ex-applicant for her own position and the most senior person in the office.

What was galling, was that after all the difficult work of turning purple prose into legally suitable language, only the Service Officer's name went on the report. And often they didn't appreciate her work. The opposite, in fact. It drove Maddie crazy. Mad, actually. And, look out world when Maddie was mad.

Because it was pure scut work. And the darling young probation Service Officers only saw their precious reports – over which they had slaved – being reduced to plain English.

"You said you'd confront her." Wayne shot a glance at his wife.

"No opportunity."

Wayne had never confronted anyone in his entire life. But he loved hearing how others could do so. Especially Maddie.

"The time will come," she said.

"That bitch has just got her knickers in a twist because she knows you should have been appointed, not her."

"I can only hope."

"He's right, Mum," Jade said, looking up from her meal to break into the conversation. "You got to have it out with her. Otherwise, you're a mouse. She's walking all over you."

"Probably fancies you like stink," Wayne said with a smirk.

Maddie was sick of them goading her into doing something she fully intended doing anyway. But timing was everything. "Who wants a sweet? I've got some ice cream in the freezer."

"I'm done," Jade said, pushing away from the table.

"After the dishes, you're done," Maddie said.

"Practicing standing up for yourself?" Jade asked, sarcasm dripping from her blackened lips. "You'll never win with me. You know that." She flounced out the room and clumped upstairs, her studied lethargy apparently forgotten.

"Jade…"

"Leave her be. She's pissed off because she was sent home to change her shoes."

"Don't tell me: she wore her trainers to school again."

"Nope. Her hiking boots."

Maddie couldn't help it. She laughed.

Chapter Three

On arriving into work the next day, Maddie looked at her schedule. One repeat arsonist who was a talkative pain. One recidivist burglar, boring. Morning meeting with the b... with Romania and other senior Probation Officers: a training session with the green-as-grass psychologist who apparently knows everything there is to know about criminal behaviour. Then Henry-the-child-molester in the afternoon. A pleasure. She knew she shouldn't have favourites, but reality meant all Probation Officers did. Or the opposite, like the stupid man who kept lighting fires so he could fantasise despicable things, the very things he loved telling Maddie about in gross detail. Lucky he was first. She could then wash her hands thoroughly after their session and forget about him.

She girded her loins (or so the saying goes) for Lawrence Reilly, the fire lighter with the obsessive sexual fantasies. Lawrence – such a soft name for such a despicable man. Today, she was determined to get more out of him than his appalling fantasies. How had he arrived at this point? He had been married, had two children, but he now was alone, living in a rough room near the wood-yard where he worked. At least he had a job. Probably fantasized how he could burn down the wood-yard. She mentally slapped her hand. No, today she was going to delve a little bit deeper.

He sat down opposite her. A small man. Scrawny but with a small pot belly. Most likely on the edge of starvation, maintained by fast-food carbs. She knew he was 47 but he looked far older. Rough hands with dirty fingernails. Unshaven. Thank goodness he'd stuck to his promise to wear trousers. She'd had problems with him wearing the shortest of shorts so he could touch himself when talking about his fantasies. So disgusting, Maddie had insisted he would not be seen, in fact would be in danger of being thrown back into prison to serve out his sentence incarcerated, if he ever, ever touched himself in the Probation Offices again. Plus, he would threaten his freedom unless he wore trousers. Everywhere. At work, at home and definitely at the Probation Office.

Maddie usually started conversations with her clients by asking how things had gone over the time since they'd last met. That, of course, meant Lawrence had an opening to talk about his fantasies, what triggered them and what he'd done about each and every one of them. Not today.

"Hello, Lawrence. To start with, I'd like to ask you about your marriage. How old were you when you got married?" She could see she'd startled him. Not what he expected.

"Twenty-two. Never been with a girl before Sal. I thought all my Christmases, you know. She was lovely. I was the happiest man alive when we got married."

"Did you have the fantasies back then?"

"No. Not a one. A golden time, Mrs Brooks, I can tell you."

"And your marriage lasted until when?"

"Not long after I got out of hospital. Had myself an injury at work."

"Why did you break up?"

"These things. I told you I can't help it." His voice wavered. "Lost Sal. She couldn't take it. Lost my kids. Not seen them in years. It's not like I want to be like this."

"So the sexual obsessions only started after you got out of hospital?"

"I wasn't supposed to live," he said with some pride in his voice. "They turned off the machines. And, guess what? I started to breathe. All by myself. Didn't wake for a while though."

Maddie searched her memory. She'd read nothing about a serious accident. One in which there was undoubted brain damage. No hospital intensive care unit turns off a life-saving machine without serious lack of brain activity, especially in a young person. "How long were you unconscious, Lawrence?"

"Three months, seventeen days." Again, pride in his voice. "The doctors said I was a miracle."

"Head injury." She said it as a statement.

"But here I am," he said with a smile.

Yes, here he was. Living in poverty on his own with horrible obsessions that, on acting them out, got him a long prison sentence. But a history of a head injury? "When did you last go to the doctor, Lawrence?"

"Dunno. I move around a bit. You know. Not easy to have a doctor."

"What about the specialists? Your neurologist?"

He shrugged. "Haven't seen him in years."

"What hospital? Who was your main doctor?"

She gathered all of the details. What if this aberration was medical in origin? What if there was some treatment?

Once Lawrence had left, she rang for more information. Official records. They'd be sent.

· · · · ●· ● · · · ·

But seeing her other client convicted of a sexual crime was different. After they had got to know each other when he was assigned to Maddie, Henry Macgregor told her very quietly that he had not molested little Geneva. Maddie nodded and smiled; so many of her crims claimed they'd been wrongly incarcerated, she'd almost expected the denial. Of course, each of her crims had had to pretend to be remorseful to the parole board or they would not have been awarded their parole, but, confidentially, they had not dunnit.

Which meant Maddie paid Henry-the-child-molester's story little heed.

However, she got along with him well. He was a former school teacher who had been convicted of sexual violation of a twelve-year-old girl, to wit, forcing her into oral sex. Enough to make anyone nauseous. He must have hit a judge with a particularly sensitive stomach or an enhanced antipathy for that sort of behaviour as he'd been given a whopping nine years. Henry's time in prison had not been happy.

In spite of the bullying to which he was subjected, Henry had survived his imprisonment without a blemish on his record. He'd spent much of his time teaching literacy skills in the prison library to those in need. He'd enjoyed some popularity there, most likely due to his undoubted pedagogical skills plus legendary patience. He'd served half of his sentence before coming before the parole board. But he had been approved and later assigned to a senior Probation Officer in the person of Madeleine Brooks.

"My goodness," Maddie said that afternoon as Henry walked in, looking different from his usual casual self.

He grinned. "My new rags. Necessary because I treated Fiona to lunch at a fancy restaurant today." He was wearing a suit and tie. And the outfit sat well on him. "Courtesy of a charity shop in

Kingston." He sat in the parolee's chair in front of Maddie's desk.

"Still banned from the wedding itself?"

"Not Fiona's idea. It's just a way my ex can get at me once again. Bloody woman," he said. "Sorry, but what mother bans a father from his daughter's wedding? I should have been walking down the aisle with her to give her away." Henry's wife had been horribly mortified, angered and made bitter by his conviction.

"As if giving away a daughter means anything," Maddie interjected.

He smiled again. "There is that. Fiona had a barny with her mother about it all. I'm sorry about that, but the woman should know Fiona and I get along well again in spite of her significant efforts to keep us apart." When Henry had been sentenced to prison for years to come, his wife paid the considerable fees charged by the barrister from their savings and then proceeded to spend the rest on clothes, holidays and restaurants. With a vengeance. Her part of their savings, she said. His went on legal fees. Fair's fair. When the money ran out, she divorced him.

"It's not unusual after a sex crime conviction."

"I almost think she was the one who set me up."

"Come on, Henry. You know better than that."

"Yes, okay. Let's change the subject. Fiona is looking radiant. Isn't that what you say about a happy bride?"

"Absolutely. And you are looking suitably spiffy."

"This suit, tie and shirt cost me far less than the lunch," he said. "I've grown to love charity shops."

"Me too," Maddie said.

"Now I have something decent to wear when I'm going out."

Maddie had been encouraging Henry to join organisations, to attend meetings, to exercise in the open air, all for both his mental and physical well-being after his incarceration. "Have you joined anything yet?"

"No. But I intend taking your advice, Mrs Brooks. It will be easier now I have something decent to wear. I think I'll go to church this Sunday. And I'll definitely join a book club at the library. It will soon be a group of little old ladies and me. Also, I've met the Chair of the local Genealogy Society who is encouraging me to join their organisation. And I do intend taking myself out for walks, although that doesn't involve dressing up. Started today with a good walk into Kingston."

"Excellent, Henry." She was truly pleased he was progressing so well at integrating himself back into society. She glanced at the topics she'd jotted down to cover with him. "Now how's the volunteer job going?"

Henry was a trained and experienced teacher. But he was now banned from teaching school-aged children, of course. Their plan was for him eventually to get a job teaching in adult education, probably English to immigrants or foreign potential students who needed better English comprehension skills before applying to university. He was starting off by volunteering at the African Peoples Society in London where he was teaching reading skills to illiterate political refugees. Adults only.

"Got another bright one assigned to me. From Somalia and tall as a basketball centre. He'd been to school when he was a child but he cannot read beyond a 7-year-old level. I started him on a simple science book about insects, of all things, and he'd mastered it within a few days. Off to a flying start." He grinned. "To coin a phrase."

"Are you keeping the journal?" She'd asked him to tally what he'd achieved each day.

"Mostly. I forget some days, but I do catch up before the memories fade. It's actually fun to read through."

"Some time in the future it'll prove useful when you need to remember what you've been doing. Like when you need details when applying for jobs. Talking of jobs, any more potentials come up?"

"Not yet. But these are early days."

Maddie laughed. "That's my line." She sobered. "And how are you in yourself, Henry?"

He looked down at his hands. "Getting by, Mrs Brooks. It's funny living by myself. But the little flat's working out just fine." He'd been lucky enough to buy a minuscule bachelor's flat so he didn't have to rent or share, paid for by his half of the amount of money raised by selling the family home. He'd felt it was money well spent as the new place was his and his alone.

"Contacted any of your former friends?"

"Don't go on about that, please, Mrs Brooks. If I'd been convicted of robbing a bank, or even of killing somebody, I could do so. Not with the offence I supposedly committed."

"Okay. How about making any new friends?"

"Do my students count?"

"Of course. And any colleagues at African Peoples, neighbours, whoever."

He paused. "I get along well with my students. Ditto my colleagues. No invitations for a drink after work, though. And I eat my lunches alone."

"Changing where you eat is within your capabilities."

He shrugged.

"Your homework for this coming week, Mr Macgregor, is to sit at least once with someone else while eating your lunch."

"They mostly buy their lunches."

"Are you grumbling?" she asked.

He shot her a glance and grinned. "Sorry. And okay, I'll figure something out. Or die trying."

"Don't go that far," Maddie said, standing up to indicate their meeting was at an end. "Same time, a fortnight from now? And we'll concentrate on whether you've become an emerging social butterfly or not."

He smiled. "It will be a pleasure," he said, bowing formally and tipping an imaginary hat.

Maddie opened the door to her office to usher him out only to find two policemen sitting in the waiting room. They rose, their eyes on Henry.

"Henry Macgregor, I'm here to bring you in for questioning," the larger of the detectives said.

"What?" he asked. "Why?"

"Come with us." He escorted Henry towards the door of the building.

The other policeman nodded at Maddie.

"What's going on?" she asked him before he could turn away.

"A child was killed this morning," he said, "not far from Macgregor's flat. The inspector wants to question him. Of course."

Maddie nodded. Of course. Any nearby sex offenders on the infamous list would be questioned. She turned to the others. "See you in a fortnight, Henry," she called.

He didn't answer.

From the Probation Service doorway, Maddie watched Henry being put into the back seat of the police car. His eyes were downcast, not looking at Maddie. She watched the car until it turned the corner. Time to ring her contact there, DI Ethan de Roque.

Not available.

She should have expected that. He was probably interviewing, not just Henry, but every child sex offender on the local list. She'd try him later, when she'd become so screamingly frustrated by the report re-writing, she'd need something to distract her attention.

But Henry's plight wasn't so easily dismissed from her mind. She found it difficult to settle down to the paperwork. The particular report she was attempting to re-write was wordy in the extreme. At least no exclamation marks this time. But she was finding it difficult to understand what the Service Officer was on about. She read and re-read the amateurish report on her screen. And had an idea.

She walked over to the appropriate desk. "I'm having trouble again, Agatha. I need your help."

The young woman nodded. Wary. "Tell me," she said.

"The Conway report has to be shorter. Considerably. The first thing I want you to do is to cut the introduction to 150 words."

She pulled up the report onto her screen. "I have no idea how long it is," she said.

"Almost 400 words. This is what you do. Make an outline of the bare bones that must be included and email it to me. Say, in half an hour? At least before you leave."

It was already almost four. If this worked, she'd do the same with the three other Service Officers. And read them at home.

Agatha wasn't best pleased, but not complaining aloud. "So, this is what you want in the future? An intro of 150 words?"

"One fifty, max, thanks, Agatha. I had to learn how to write reports the hard way. We'll get there together without you losing face in the courts as happened to me."

Agatha gave her a worried smile.

Her colleagues had much the same reaction. Good, that left Maddie clear to ring her tame DI again.

"Don't get your knickers in a twist, Madeleine. It's almost routine," de Roque said. "The questioning is precautionary given Macgregor's proximity to where the child was found."

"So he's not under arrest?"

"I'll need you to recall him for a month. He's here at the moment, but I'd prefer he's transferred out to prison soon."

"He denied everything?"

"Of course," de Roque said, "as expected with his history. Clever shite, though. And I don't trust clever shites."

"I saw him today," Maddie said. "No red flags at the time. I'll come and see him in about an hour."

"No prob. He's downstairs. You can see him whenever you get here."

By four-forty-five, she had emails from each of the four Service Officers containing their outlines and a summons to Romania's office.

"What are you thinking?" she began when Maddie closed the door. "I gave you a simple task because our Service Officers are over-worked. You can crank out reports at ten times the speed."

"And so will they, once I've trained them."

"This is not a training institution."

"All work places are training institutions for new employees."

"I'm warning you," Romania spluttered, "one more complaint from a Service Officer and you're in deep doo-doo."

Maddie stared at her, wheeled around and left the office.

Doo-doo, indeed.

Chapter Four

Maddie asked for Henry to be brought up to an interview room, kindly made available on the orders of DI de Roque. It was late in the day. The visit would be short.

She hardly recognised the defeated looking man ushered into the room and unceremoniously dumped onto a chair at the small metal table.

"Henry, it's not as bad as it feels. DI de Roque has to interview every sex offender, with a priority of every paedophilic offender on the list. You know that. You will have to go to prison until this is cleared up. Don't worry, I'm on your case and I don't want you in prison for one unneeded day, all right?"

He nodded, his eyes still downcast.

"But the body of the child who died was found in the Thames not far from your block of flats."

"My flat's not that near the river," he murmured. "There's a road, quite a big embankment, the towpath and a strip of bushes and trees on the riverbank. I love the view, but it's more than a few minutes' walk to the water."

"The paths, some of them cross the grassland not far from you, don't they? And you'd know the area now."

"I walk there lots, yes. As do masses of people, especially those of us in tiny flats."

She frowned.

"Don't look at me like that. I used to walk to Horscliffe a lot when I was a teacher there. About a twenty minute walk from my old house. A little less from the flat, I'd guess. But I used to walk along the towpath for part of the way. A little longer route, but more attractive. So, yes, I know the area. It's not close to the school. Besides, you know how I had to jump through all the hoops when I wanted to buy the flat. It passed all the proximity rules."

She nodded. She'd supervised the process. "Kids play there?"

"Lots of them do. Kids on bikes and skateboards. Most with families, though. Where was the child actually found?"

"No idea. But if she walked to school that way…."

He closed his eyes and took a deep breath. "Look, Mrs Brooks, my daughter's wedding is tomorrow. Is there any way my being here can be kept out of the papers?"

She felt for him. "I don't think DI de Roque is all that concerned about you. But, to be honest, there's no way we can know what any others think. Leaks happen. You're vulnerable, for sure. We'll just have to keep fingers and toes crossed."

He didn't smile. Or sit straighter. He sighed. "Just one more day. Then they go off to Spain for their honeymoon."

"Your daughter won't hear anything from me," Maddie said, "but she's a witness about that time frame."

"Is that when the child was killed? When we were at the restaurant?" He looked up.

"At least you can prove you were in the public eye during that lunch," she said. "To answer your question, nobody has told me when she died. But that's the sort of detail that gets into the papers. I'll watch the news tonight; buy the papers in the morning. Let you know."

A knock on the door before it was pushed open. The guard to take Henry back to his cell.

Maddie rose to her feet. "I'll see you here about eight tomorrow morning if I can arrange it now."

"Thank you," he muttered, flicking his eyes briefly to Maddie's.

She caught an anguished look. Was it guilt that his sordid crime had been discovered? Or concern about spoiling his daughter's big day? Or was she noticing him feeling utterly defeated because this was a repeat of last time?

Maddie walked to her car parked behind the Probation Service building, her steps slow and almost painful.

When had her boundless enthusiasm for her job disappeared? Obvious. When Romania had taken over. No, not quite. To be brutally honest, it was when she'd heard she'd not been appointed. That meant this lethargy was not due to Romania's presence even though it was exacerbated by the woman's behaviour to her; it was merely due to her own discontent. End of an era of doing a good job that was highly appreciated.

Wayne was watching some game on television when she arrived home.

"Hello light-of-my-life," he called without taking his eyes off the screen. "What's for supper?"

"Catfood à la king," she said, half to herself as she dumped groceries onto the kitchen table.

"Sounds good," he said, still immersed in the game.

She climbed upstairs to her home office and sank into the chair in front of the computer. She'd have a quick look at the Service Officers' outlines before cooking. Pork chops, boiled spuds and broccoli. Easy and quick.

Agatha had got it. She'd produced a small outline of 63 words and had tried out how she could smooth the first point into a proper sentence. She ended her email by asking if that was what Maddie was after.

Maddie replied with an enthusiastic 'Yes!' and a request to treat the other points the same way. She suggested that Agatha search through her outline to discover whether any point could be best combined with any other point, thus organising the report intro efficiently. She hit 'send'.

The second and third Service Officers had made reasonable fists of her instructions but the fourth had not understood what Maddie was getting at. She'd turned each sentence of her verbose report into a point, all 127 of them. Was she taking the mickey? Maddie sighed and told the young woman to see her at … she glanced at her online calendar … nine-thirty the next morning. She copied and pasted Agatha's email, changed it to read as an instruction with an example, and sent a copy to both of the other Service Officers. Much better than having four deadly dull bits of prose to amend and re-write knowing full well the authors would carry on forever producing shoddy work. She gave half a second's thought to Romania's annoyance. Tough.

With a slightly lighter tread, Maddie went downstairs to start dinner. Wayne was sitting at the table biting into a large sandwich.

"Dinner will be in half an hour," she said trying to keep the irritation from her voice.

"Didn't have lunch," he said between bites.

"Couldn't you wait?"

"Didn't know it was so soon, did I? You weren't making anything."

She bit back a retort. Obviously, at almost six, dinner was due shortly. But not all dinner preparations take a long time.

"No Jade?" she asked.

"At Freya's place. Studying for English. The exam is coming up. She's been invited to stay for a meal. Salmon on the barbie."

"Lucky for some," Maddie said. Freya Dymock and Jade had been friends for a number of years. Both were going through a Goth phase, which had engendered a few phone calls back and forth between the parents. Sharon Dymock was something in women's fashion and her husband Donald, a teacher. Nice people. They lived in a large home on Ham Common, north of the main part of Kingston, the size of the property presumably due to the fashion business. Sharon was Australian and somehow had convinced Donald to take over barbecuing and it seemed he loved his barbies, no matter the weather or time of year. "So, you and me for dinner. But now, presumably, not you."

Wayne looked sheepish. "Sorry. But I was hungry. Not anymore. So don't bother about cooking for me."

Maddie stifled a sigh as she returned the chops into the fridge. She'd cook herself an omelette. "I really don't want to work in Probation anymore," she said.

"Butchy-Bitch getting at you?"

"Please, Wayne."

"Sorrrry." He drew it out.

She sighed. "Getting at me? Yes and no. Yes, today she was showing her true colours once more. No, I can take her silliness. Annoying though it is. And, no question I'm frustrated because of her incompetence. But she's not responsible for my attitude right now. Mostly, anyway." It was as if she'd come to a stopping place. No way forward, just endless circling going nowhere. Romania was a blockage, no question, but it would have been anyone appointed instead of her. Her own character weakness, she concluded.

"So, no more talk about not wanting to work?"

She shot him a glance. "Why? Because you'd have to get a job?"

"Don't turn it onto me, Madeleine Brooks. You know damn well we have a mortgage to pay. No more talk about quitting your job, okay?"

Maddie got up to do the dishes, turning her back on her husband.

Chapter Five

Henry was already in the interview room when Maddie arrived shortly after eight. If she was condemned to circling, she'd damn well do it on her terms. From this moment on.

"Your papers, sir," she said with a smile as she piled three newspapers onto the table. "And, to cut to the chase, not a word about you."

Henry's worried expression lightened. "And telly?"

"Nothing. Nix. Nada." She grinned at him. "So far, so good. What time is the wedding?"

"Three this afternoon. Followed by photography in the park and the wedding reception after that. They should be on their way by about ten or eleven tonight, I suppose."

"That probably means flying out tomorrow morning." Her grin faded. Another twenty-four hours before the newlyweds were safely away.

He was obviously thinking the same. "Maybe she'll be so excited, she won't be noticing any of the news." His face darkened again. "But if her mother has even a smell of what's happening...."

"Walk me through yesterday, Henry, please." She asked him as much to get his mind off his daughter as for the information she wanted to know.

"Got up, had breakfast, headed for Mr Bazir's magazine shop in Kingston to pay my newspaper bill. I waited for the bus for a bit – the bus stop is just outside my flat – but I'd probably just missed one so decided to walk instead. I needed to get to Kingston, you see, because I intended buying a suit for the lunch with my daughter."

"Buying a suit? Don't you have suits from before you went to prison?"

"I had several. All donated to my favourite charity shop. They'll fit a much larger man than me at my new slimmer weight. Of course, they fitted perfectly before I went away. Prison food had an unanticipated but welcome consequence."

She smiled. "Got it. But why did you leave it so late? Shouldn't you have done that sort of shopping earlier in the week?"

"I've been going into Kingston every chance I get, seeing what new stock the charity shops have acquired, almost buying but waiting in case anything better came in. I'd checked them all out yesterday except my fav charity shop, the hospice shop, near the underpass. That was the last chance for a suit with a good fit."

"I know the shop."

"I did try to buy a brand new suit. First, I'd checked out Marks and Sparks, the sales at John Lewis, that sort of thing. Needless to say, the High Street shops were way beyond my current budget. After that, I went several times to four local charity shops to look at the quality of the suits, whether any fitted me and their prices. I did find two almost good enough suits. But they were nothing like the one I ended up buying. At a pinch, either would have done, but neither excited me at all. Last shop to check was the one near the underpass. My fav charity shop, for sure. Where I'd donated my other suits."

"If it had been me, I'd have gone there first."

"I've been several times. In fact, I'd tried on a suit there earlier in the week. It fitted perfectly but was a bit old fashioned and it was brown. Not the greatest colour for lunching with my daughter. But a fit is a fit. Anyway, overnight, a new suit had come in. Charcoal grey with a hint of blue. Could have been tailored for me, don't you think?"

"Absolutely. A good buy?"

"Twelve quid. Then another two for the shirt and tie. Actually, Kathy threw in the tie."

"Kathy?"

"She volunteers there. Also why I left that particular shop until she'd be there. She's a pet, is Kathy."

"Did you notice the time?"

"Not when I got there, but Fiona was picking me up at half eleven, early enough so we would have plenty of time to find a parking space. And enough time to walk to the restaurant for our reservations at noon. All the faffing around with Kathy and the suit probably took an hour, I suppose. Working back, Fiona picked me up on time. I had just finished my cup of coffee in the café across from the charity shop. So, maybe twenty minutes or so having coffee? That's back to 11:10. An hour before that, I probably got to the hospice shop. That would be, say, 10:10. I wanted to time my arrival when Kathy was working and her hours are ten to four."

Maddie was jotting it all down in a small notebook she carried everywhere in her handbag. "Sounds good. Lots of people would have seen you, presumably."

"Didn't notice, but I assume so. Okay, before that: I'd estimate walking from Mr Bazir's shop to the charity shop was, say, five minutes or so – before that, about ten minutes with him as he fussed around, we chatted and I paid my paper bill. The walk into Kingston takes about half an hour. So, something before nine thirty when I was going into Mr Bazir's? I'd waited for the bus a bit of time, though. Maybe ten minutes? I'd left the flat at half eight, maybe a bit later, so we only have about 20 minutes not accounted for. Something like that, anyway."

"Unless the child was killed very early in the morning."

"Yes." His face clouded again.

He looked at her. "You're helping, Mrs Brooks. Truly."

"Helping?"

"Easing my mind. Going over my morning like this. And I know I didn't murder any young girl. But when we list what I did yesterday, it was pretty much full. And I can say that with confidence now."

"It eases my mind too, of course," Maddie said. She tucked the notebook away. "I have to get into work." She rose.

"Could I ask a big favour?"

"Ask. If I can, I'll help."

"Fiona and I were going straight to the restaurant so I dressed in the suit and tie with no time to nip home. I had to leave the clothes I was wearing with Kathy at the charity shop. If I don't pick them up, they might get added to the gear they're selling in the shop and I've lost them. I told her I'd pick them up today."

"No problem," Maddie said. "I'll pop over later and collect them."

Which she did. After an interminable meeting Romania had organised to write a mission statement for their office. A mission statement. Who said they were missionaries…?

During her lunch break, Maddie walked to the hospice shop which took her fifteen minutes or so. She strode out, feeling how good it felt to stretch her legs and breathe some fresh air.

The shop had a tiny frontage but expanded into a spacious shop behind. How different these modern charity shops were to the horrible and smelly second-hand shops of yore. She asked the elderly woman manning the till if a 'Kathy' was working today.

"In the back. I'll just get her."

Maddie moved over to look at the jewellery. She noticed an amber coloured necklace. Two pounds. Probably plastic. Nice colours, though. Each bead subtly different. Did that mean they could be the real deal?

The elderly woman reappeared with a middle aged woman behind, smiling at her uncertainly.

"You're Kathy?" Maddie asked, then noticing a large name tag above her left breast.

"Kathy Milhouse. Can I help?"

"I'm here to pick up the clothes Henry Macgregor left here yesterday morning. He's indisposed today and is afraid his gear will become mixed up with donations."

"Henry? Henry Who?"

"He bought a beautiful suit, shirt and tie yesterday to take his daughter out to lunch."

"My goodness, of course. I'm not sure he ever told me his name. Yes, he left his clothes under the payment desk. I'll just pop them into a bag for you." She refolded each item and placed them into a large paper bag. "He's not unwell, is he?"

"He'll be fine. But he was worried about losing his clothes."

As Maddie walked back, her mood had lightened. Henry's story held. And, somehow, she knew it would. She'd have to let DI de Roque know a witness existed for a decent chunk of the morning, and that Henry left the shop already dressed in the suit and tie he'd just purchased. Also, it occurred to her his other clothes could be of interest, perhaps, in any police inquiry. If they were as clean as they appeared to be, they'd also be vital to his defence.

At the end of the day, she called into the police station to tell Henry she had his clothes. It was just before five and she was allowed down to the cells.

"Nothing in the news?"

"Nothing." She smiled at him.

"They'll be having cocktails now, at the reception."

"And having a grand time."

He smiled. "My fingers and toes are all still crossed."

After seeing Henry, Maddie popped into DI de Roque's office. "He says he was buying those fancy clothes in a charity shop yesterday morning. I can confirm it. I talked to the volunteer saleswoman. He left his other clothes there and I've now got them."

"I'll take them."

"Fine." She scrutinised his face. Passive. "Or do you want me to keep them for him?"

"He's still a person of interest, Madeleine. And remember to call me Ethan."

"Sorry. Ethan. Will you test the clothes?"

He just looked at her.

"Okay. I'll fetch them from my car."

When Maddie returned to work, a well-stuffed A4 envelope had been delivered. She emptied it out on her desk. Sheaves of paper about one person, Lawrence Reilly.

She read the accompanying letter and skimmed the medical reports. He had been unconscious for over three months, as he had claimed. Many of the reports concerned his rehabilitation which took over a year. But he was finally pronounced fit to return to work. Early on, his boss had informed the family that Lawrence's job was awaiting his recovery. His word was good and Lawrence started half time, gradually increasing to full time as a labourer in the wood-yard. The last report was seven years ago.

Her phone rang.

Romania.

"Bring in those reports."

Maddie was startled. "Pardon me?"

"Do I have to repeat myself? Come here with those reports."

Maddie picked up the rehabilitation reports, shoving them into the brown manila envelope. The covering letter and medical summaries went into her drawer. No way was she losing those. But the reports? She'd show her boss those.

She walked into Romania's presence. Romania was looking at her screen. Without looking at Maddie, she held out one hand. "Thank you," she said.

"Would you like to know what this is about?"

"I'm sure it will be self-explanatory."

Maddie's brain galloped from one possibility to another. Someone must have said she'd received a stuffed envelope. And Romania used the word 'report' generically. Pure nosiness. Micro-managing everything Maddie was doing. No trust at all in Maddie's abilities.

Maddie stood, quietly seething, while Romania transferred her attention from her screen to the envelope. She skim-read the top report – speech therapy, if Maddie remembered correctly. Romania then flicked from one report to another.

"Physiotherapy, speech therapy, occupational therapy," Maddie said. "He must have had quite an injury."

"No psychological report?"

"It's there somewhere." She hoped so. Of course, it could be in the lot inside her drawer.

"Look, get the psych report. It's Erin's domain. And this is junk." She impatiently jammed the papers back into the envelope. "Don't waste any time on it."

Maddie took that as a dismissal and scooted out the door. When she was on the other side, she tugged her forelock. One of the Service Officers saw her.

"Jes' obeyin' orders," Maddie said.

"As one should," the young woman said, then winked.

They all knew Romania by now.

"Erin in?"

"At the mo. But she's on duty at the prison this afternoon and she'll be leaving soon."

Maddie hurried to the psychologist's small office. At least she had an office to herself. She knocked. "Erin?"

"Hi Maddie – look, I'm just off. Almost late."

"This will take seconds. Lawrence Reilly?"

"Getting nowhere with him. All he talks about…"

"I know. Same, same. But I've just found out he survived a massive head injury. Got the details. The obsessions didn't start until afterwards."

"Wow," she said. She was young. Fully trained and, with a few years of experience, she'd be quite good one day.

"I'll fill you in when you have some time."

"Perfect," Erin said. "Thanks."

"Can I use your office this afternoon?"

"Be my guest." And she was away.

Maddie sat in glorious isolation, reading through the rehab reports with interest. A slow recovery, with several setbacks, but eventually he made it. Obviously the therapists were all fond of him and going the extra mile to see him right. No psych report.

After she heard Romania's voice – she did have a voice that carried – telling the office she was required in court, Maddie scuttled back to her own desk to get the rest of the papers.

She re-read the covering letter. From the neurologist. Worried that they had lost track of Lawrence. Now this notification from Probation meant he had been in trouble. Could Maddie see that Lawrence came into the clinic next week? He'd appreciate it.

Maddie made a note to contact Lawrence to see if he could get time off work. And she decided to make sure he got to the appointment.

Next she read the first of the medical reports. Horrific reading. Lawrence, working outside in a noisy wood-yard, had been struck from behind by a load swung by a crane. They got him into hospital quickly where a team operated, removing blood clots from in and around his brain and eventually sewing up his scalp.

She read about the decision-making about the turning off of his life support. The consultations with what the neurologist described as a 'loving family'. All were agreed. The machines turned off. But Lawrence breathed on, much to the amazement of everyone. He remained unconscious, eventually being transferred to a long term facility. When he first showed signs of consciousness returning, the neurologist was hesitant. Told the family there may be deep and permanent brain damage. Difficulty doing things, even walking. Probable intellectual damage. Most likely personality changes. In other words, not the man they'd known and loved.

Intellectual? Maddie skipped back. What position did Lawrence hold before the accident? She found it in the occupational therapist's report: supervisor. So there had been intellectual damage. Maddie had noticed Lawrence occasionally used vocabulary that surprised her. Such as never utilising euphemisms for his erection, but always calling it as such. Talking about having an excess of testosterone, used and pronounced correctly. Remnants of his past intelligence.

Pity welled up inside her. This man had been in the corrections system for years and years without anyone doing anything. Misjudging him. Something must be done.

· · ● ● ● ● ● · · ·

Dinnertime was quiet. Maddie had objected to Jade having her ear buds in, resulting in compliance with a thunderous face. Wayne kept out of it, just shovelling her tasty chicken cacciatore into his maw without comment or appreciation.

"Are we a family or random people eating at a fast food joint?" Her exasperation spilled into the tone of her words. She remembered the meals they used to have. Before Jade's Goth period, before Olivia was married. Good conversation. Scintillating at times. Both girls participating. Wayne sometimes yelling in excitement while getting his ideas across. How long since that had occurred?

"Sorry," Wayne said. "Head otherwise engaged."

Jade flicked her eyes up, sighed, and bent down over her food again.

"Look, I'm sure we have each had something that happened today that will be of interest to one or the other of us. Surely."

"Yeah, I suppose so," Wayne said, frowning. "Me first. My mixer is hopelessly out of date. I went online to see what I could get to replace it. Lots of good stuff available. Pricey, of course. But everything in the music field is pricey." He snatched a look at Maddie.

She concentrated on not reacting. Hinting he needed yet another piece of equipment? He always wanted to replace what he had. Always with something better. But she put on a smile. "Fun stuff, looking at potential, isn't it."

"I'll put it on my Christmas Wish List," he said, having caught the underlying message.

"Jade?" Maddie asked.

"Nothing."

"Anything, Jade. Just a small contribution, thirty seconds only … no, even ten seconds will do."

Jade sighed with as much exaggeration as she could muster. "Freya forgot to do her English homework; Miss Jenkins had an epi. Said she'd tell on her to Freya's dad. Freya said for her to go ahead."

Maddie searched for a non-preachy reaction. "She'll be in trouble at home?"

Jade shrugged. "Probably not. Jenks has the hots for Donald. He basks in the attention. Probably the whole thing was an excuse for Jenks to have a cosy little chat with him."

Maddie glanced at Wayne who was studying his forkful of food.

"Yes, well, interesting. I'm not sure you should be calling Mr Dymock 'Donald', though."

"He told me to. At home, of course." Head down again.

"What if you forget at school?"

"Come on, Mum. As if."

Maddie took a deep breath. "My turn. Mine was a small thing too. But curious and could be important. Maybe." She glanced at them both. And had the satisfaction of momentary, at least, glances back. "I have a client in jail right now accused of something rather horrible. But I checked and a vital part of his alibi has been corroborated."

"Like, how?" Jade asked.

"He said he was in a second-hand shop and the person who served him remembered him well. Such a relief."

Jade looked at her dad. "As if we don't know what horrible crime the guy was accused of, eh, Dad?"

"Don't have a clue," Wayne muttered.

Jade sniffed. "The murder. Of course. The girl from Year 7 who got killed. Nothing else has happened that you'd think was horrible."

"Don't expect me to confirm it," Maddie said, annoyed she'd given enough away that Jade clued in directly. "And keep your speculations to yourself, okay?"

At that Wayne's head shot up. "Your mother's in hot water at work. So, no blabbing. We don't want her losing her job."

"All right, already," Jade said. She turned to her mother. "I actually think it's cool you did that for him."

"Cool. Yes, good word," Maddie said, with a flash of affection for this difficult daughter of hers.

That evening, Maddie looked over the new introductions to the four reports. Three were acceptable and Agatha had gone on to re-write her entire report, now shrunk to almost half the size of her first attempt.

Maddie tweaked the two introductions written by the other two Service Officers using track changes so they could see clearly what she was altering and emailed them back with a 'well done!' and asked them to have an attempt at using the same technique for the rest of the report. She then concentrated on Agatha's report, made a few amendments, also using track changes, and emailed it back congratulating her on this version and giving her permission to submit it. The fourth, however, was a headache.

Time was running out, so she buckled down to do the hated re-write of the report.

Once finished, she emailed, "Hi Daniella – I have rewritten your original report this time. For the next, would you please consult with Agatha before starting it? Maybe you could suggest writing your reports together. As she will tell you, court reports have to be short and concise using specific language. Good luck."

Her theory was that Agatha was still learning and thus not so far above Daniella's level to be daunting. But she'd have to talk to Agatha, maybe persuade her.

· · · · ● · ● · · ·

The next morning, Maddie had a message from Ethan that Henry Macgregor had been transferred back to prison. Wandsworth, this time. She sent an email to Henry there, telling him she would send him any news by email if she felt he needed to know anything. She ended it with, 'Keep smiling.' Difficult to know what to say to someone returned to prison on the basis of suspicion although, so far, no evidence. She knew not to expect an answer back. Prisoners can receive messages, not reply.

At least the transfer had been routine. Hopefully, the newlyweds were out of the country by now.

Her new determination to do what she felt was best had persisted. It still felt good.

If it got her fired, so be it.

Chapter Six

The story broke that afternoon on television news. Henry Macgregor, convicted child sex offender, had been returned to prison in light of the murder of the thirteen-year-old schoolgirl, Linsey Benton. He'd been convicted five years before of a child sexual offence but paroled recently.

The morning papers were full of it. Righteous indignation that a sex offender was released on parole. Diatribes against the system that allowed these monsters into our communities. Apparently, he lived near where the child was found. Linsey Benton was a pupil at Horscliffe, the school where he used to teach, the same school his previous victim had attended. Jade's school. It all sounded ghastly and apparently provided a slam-dunk for his guilt.

Morning talk shows featured people's opinions that sex offenders should have electronic bracelets so the police knew where they were at any time; should be locked up forever; should be executed; maybe hanged, drawn and quartered – always something that kept them away from the community. While driving in, Maddie listened to enough of it to renew her antipathy against populism. She turned the ignorant voices off well before she arrived. Besides, she knew she'd be questioned as soon as she got in and she had to decide how to play it.

"Did he do it?" her friend and colleague Caroline texted.

"My instinct is no, but what do I know? I've been wrong before."

Several others asked as well. More were listening to the various exchanges. As expected.

Agatha was one of them. "The boss wants to see you." Again, as expected.

"Thanks. I'll go in as soon as I get a cup of tea." Delaying tactics, but several of her little audience nodded. It's what they would have done in her shoes.

"Sit down," Romania said as Maddie walked in with her fresh cup of tea. "Explain to me every little detail about this sex offender you've returned to prison."

"Starting where?"

"His offence. The original one."

Maddie bridled inwardly but kept her face passive. She hoped so, anyway. She wanted to pick her arguments carefully with this woman, not rise to the bait willy-nilly. That was the idea, anyway.

"The child was … is Geneva Hopworth. She was twelve at the time. In her first year at secondary school. Maybe about 4:30 in the afternoon and it was dark by then. Winter. She was half way home when she realised she'd forgotten her shoes at the gym, so she retraced her steps. The school should have been locked up, but the door nearest the gym was open. She said she went into the changing rooms to find her shoes.

"Her mother arrived home by 5:15 as usual. She described Geneva as withdrawn and quiet. Didn't eat much dinner. Watched television for a while then took herself off to bed early. These things were unusual for her daughter. In the morning, Geneva refused to go to school. She wouldn't tell her mother why. Mother annoyed and insisted. Once there, Geneva took herself to the nurse's office and spent the day by herself sleeping on the nurse's cot, saying she hadn't slept much the night before. Wouldn't tell the nurse any specifics. When home after school, she still didn't eat properly. At midnight, the mother found Geneva sobbing in the kitchen. Her story came tumbling out."

Romania sighed. "Get on with it."

"This is what happened, Romania. Do you want me to continue?"

"A little less of the sobbing child and more of what actually took place."

Maddie took a deep breath. "Geneva said she entered the girls' changing rooms and spotted her shoes. As she walked over to them, a naked man came out of the showers. She screamed. She said it was Mr Macgregor. Henry Macgregor. So far, the stories of both Geneva and Macgregor coincide. He was having a shower at the school before going out to dinner."

"In the girls' changing rooms?"

"The school was all locked up. Nobody else was there."

"Except it wasn't, and someone was."

"He insisted he checked."

"Go on," Romania said.

"The girl wanted to leave but Macgregor wouldn't let her. Insisted on oral sex which he proceeded to inflict on the child. Finally he let her leave after threatening if she told, he'd say she came onto him. And, by the way, he dropped her shoes off at the 'lost property' office the next day."

"What?"

"That's one of the strange things, yes," Maddie said.

"DNA?"

"No. Too long afterwards. Besides, he was naked and her school uniform had been washed."

"But he was convicted. Any witnesses?"

"A mother and her son saw a girl outside of the school. And only one car in the school carpark that was obviously Macgregor's. They couldn't say precisely when they saw the child and the car, but knew it was before five."

"Nothing to corroborate Macgregor's story?"

"He was having dinner with three friends. They all said he arrived on time, seemed to enjoy the dinner, left about ten o'clock. Was his usual social self. None of them saw anything abnormal."

"The child was a good witness, then." A statement, not a query.

"Geneva had detailed memories of the fellatio. In her evidentiary interview, she described how she felt she was choking. How he was holding her head. The stuff of nightmares. I guess it provided overwhelming proof to the jury."

"What did he get?"

"Nine years."

"A long time, longer than most."

"I guess we all felt that. The judge was obviously disbelieving and horrified that the man was a teacher."

"Can't disagree, right?"

Maddie didn't answer. She changed the subject instead. "He had an unblemished record in prison. I've arranged for him to volunteer teaching literacy skills to African immigrants. He'd taught illiterate prisoners while he was incarcerated. Excellent results in both places."

"Obviously a charmer."

"Not obviously so but he comes across as intelligent and articulate." She drained her tea. She'd given herself until then before getting out of the office.

"Sounds like you've been naïve."

Maddie shrugged and stood up. More bait. Same result: she was going to ignore it.

"And the new offence?"

"I'll talk to the police today."

"You haven't already?"

"I should have said, I'll talk to the police *again* today. So far, they haven't been forthcoming."

Romania waved her away and Maddie grabbed the opportunity before any more questions could be asked. As she left, she noticed a newspaper on the side table. If Romania had read it, she'd known as much about the current situation as Maddie did.

Once lunchtime came, Maddie walked over to the police station, the story of Henry's old crime reverberating around her head. They had treated the case as open and shut. But those two strange things bothered her then and bothered her now: his bringing the child's shoes into the lost property office the next day and his dinner companions insisting they had a leisurely and completely normal dinner together not long after the crime took place. Would a paedophile take his victim's shoes to someone, a someone he knew and with whom he had an ordinary collegial relationship? Could a paedophile be so completely at ease with what he'd just done that he could enjoy dinner with close friends so soon afterwards? Maybe, if, and only if, he was a cold-blooded psychopath. Was Henry a psychopath? She'd bank her twenty years as a Probation Officer on the negative. She spotted psychopaths easily. Especially after a conversation or two. That, or she was badly losing competence in her job.

"Anything more you can tell me about the murdered child?" she asked DI de Roque. "I've read the papers."

He sighed. "They have it mostly right. The child – her name is Linsey Benton and she was thirteen – was dropped off at Horscliffe by her mother. Several children saw Linsey leave again – they thought she'd forgotten something in the car. But she didn't return. Round about noon, a family walking along the towpath a mile or so north of the school found the child's body at the edge of the Thames, half in the water."

"Drowned?"

"So the pathologist says."

"Henry was preparing for a special lunch out and had a full and public morning. He attended the lunch in a suit and tie. I presume that means he's unlikely to be of particular interest?"

He shook his head.

"Come on, Ethan. It's me. Just spill it out, please."

"The child drowned. But she had some bruises. A couple of them were on her face. Just where somebody's thumbs would be if she was struggling while he was holding her head underwater."

"Awful." But Maddie had relaxed. "I can't imagine Henry killing a child."

Ethan stared at her. "The throat was bruised. Not outside. Inside. The child most likely had been involved in violent fellatio."

She stared back at him. "More than awful," she muttered. "And that puts Henry bang in your sights again."

"Even more so," he said.

"What was the time of death?"

"About ten-thirty / eleven. Estimate only."

"That could leave Henry in the clear. He was shopping in Kingston well before ten and constantly busy with other people through mid-afternoon."

"So he says. We've got people looking into it. The estimated time period is nine-thirty through eleven-thirty am." He dropped his eyes to the papers he had on his desk. "She was dropped off at school shortly before eight-thirty. Her teacher asked if anyone knew where she was and a couple of girls told her about Linsey's brief appearance earlier. The teacher rang the mother who got concerned and rang here. We let our people know. A car was flagged down by a distraught family a few hours later, maybe half an hour's walk north of Horscliffe School."

"Did she have any other injuries?"

"Scraped knees. A bruise on one arm."

"Hate to ask, but was she raped vaginally as well?"

"No. But she wasn't a virgin. She'd had sex recently, but not that recently."

"Thirteen."

"Yeah, I know."

Maddie turned to go. She hated child murders; child sex murders doubly so. "What about DNA?" she asked at the door.

"Don't know yet. Let's hope."

"Thanks for bringing me up to date," she said. She got as far as the outside of Ethan's office, then remembered her consternation about Henry's mental state. "Can we find out whether Macgregor saw a psychologist when he was in prison?"

"I'll ask. Why?"

"He doesn't come across as psychopathic."

"Evil comes in lots of guises," Ethan said, tidying the papers on his desk.

"Probably, but these two crimes both smack of psychopathy."
He shrugged.

· · · ● ● · ● ● · · ·

Lawrence came in. As requested, he had showered, shaved and looked respectable in clean jeans, t-shirt and jacket.

"You coming with me?" he asked Maddie.

"I'll take you there. They're expecting you. But I will wait for you and run you back here afterwards. How's that?"

He nodded, clearly nervous. "I should have gone back, shouldn't I?"

"Probably," Maddie answered easily. "But they are not angry at you, Lawrence. They are really pleased you are coming in for this appointment."

"Okay." But he sat picking at his fingernails the whole ride in.

When they arrived, Maddie sat in the waiting room while Lawrence disappeared for his appointment. Later, to her surprise, she was called in.

"Dr Singh," the doctor said as he extended his hand to her. "I was the one who wrote to you. Thank you for bringing in Mr Reilly. He's done amazingly well. But when I asked him what trouble he was in, he said 'arson' but it was 'worse than that'. He said to bring you in to explain."

"You tell him," Lawrence said. "You'll say it better than me."

Maddie looked him in the eye. "The obsessions?"

"You can explain about them."

Maddie did. "And when he told me about his head injury," she said to Dr Singh but with a glance at Lawrence, "that provoked me to think that possibly there was something medical that could be done. And when I heard he'd been lost to you people, I was concerned. I'm very pleased you want to be still involved."

"Definitely," Dr Singh said. "We all do. A psychiatrist saw him back then. I can get her to examine Lawrence again." He turned to his patient. "That all right with you?"

"Anything that can get me free from my obsessions. It's got me into big trouble. Ruined my life."

"And I'll organise a neuro-psych evaluation. And an endocrinologist – we'll need what he has to say. We had consults from many specialists along the way – I'll put it to the team. Our Lawrence came a very long way. He must have support. We'll all gear up once more."

"Thank you, Dr Singh," Maddie said. Things were set in motion. The good old NHS.

"Thank *you*, Mrs Brooks. I'm impressed and grateful for identifying what was needed."

· · · ● ● · ● ● · · ·

"Is that your guy?" Wayne asked when the story of Henry's re-incarceration came on the news that evening. "He involved with the murder of the girl?"

"I hope not," Maddie answered. "But 'my guy' as you call him was sent down for a similar crime. Not murder, though. And murdering a child seems way beyond anything I'd thought he could or would ever do."

"When sex is involved, who knows what a guy can do."

"We know his movements almost all day. I told you I met a woman who works at a charity shop who can corroborate he bought a suit, shirt and tie. He was going out to lunch later in the day. Nice lady, Kathy. She remembers him well."

"The girls went to Horscliffe. Both of them." Jade was standing at the doorway. "The one your guy got done for, way back when. And this new one. Everyone's talking about it. Not that we knew the kid – she's way younger than us. But Freya knows her boyfriend."

Maddie swivelled to look at Jade. "A boyfriend," she said keeping her voice neutral.

"Yeah. Brody Somebody. Used to be in Freya's class in primary school a hundred years ago."

"Her age, your age?"

Jade shrugged. "S'pose. She hasn't seen him in ages."

"How old was the murdered kid, anyway?" Wayne asked.

"Thirteen," Maddie said. She turned to Jade who was climbing the stairs. "She was only thirteen, Jade. You sure her boyfriend was seventeen?"

"Seventeen or eighteen. Not sure. I'll ask Freya."

"What's an older teenager doing with a thirteen year old girlfriend?" Wayne muttered.

"Good question." And a disturbing one.

Chapter Seven

Again, Maddie found herself at the police station before work.

"The murdered child. Did you know about a boyfriend?" she asked Ethan.

"Presumed there was one, what with the pathologist's findings," he said. He was pulling his jacket on, ready to go out. "But the family doesn't know about any boyfriend. We checked."

"The kids at the school are speculating, as you can imagine," Maddie said. "The word is there was a boyfriend, all right. The boy is older. Seventeen or eighteen."

Ethan closed his eyes. "Damn. We'll have to find him. He'll never come forward voluntarily." He bent over to grab his briefcase.

"Oh, of course. Rape. Statutory rape." Maddie winced at how a reasonable law could have an unforeseeable impact on an investigation like this one.

Ethan sighed. "He'll be as close-mouthed as a toddler being fed broccoli."

She smiled. Ethan was a dad. "First name: Brody," she said. "Or so says my source."

"Who is...?"

"Schoolgirl gossip. Can we leave it at that?"

He ushered her out of his office and closed the door behind both of them. "And how's that daughter of yours doing, Maddie?"

She smiled and asked him about his two little boys and whether they liked broccoli.

• • • • • • • • • •

Maddie had to put more input into two of the Service Officer's reports than with Agatha's, but she was reasonably pleased with the efforts of all three. The fourth, Daniella, still was having problems grasping the concepts she was trying to teach, but the idea of Agatha and Daniella working on their next reports together went as well as could be expected. As a result, though, Agatha's report was honed within an inch of its existence and Daniella's was considerably better than her last one. Certainly not in the same league as the others, but requiring less input from Maddie.

Two days later, she was partially re-writing Daniella's report in the evening when Wayne came up to her home office.

"Not still holding those little amateurs' hands, are you?"

Maddie looked up, irritated. She was allowed to make disparaging remarks about the Service Officers, not him. "Huge improvements, Wayne. I can see the light at the end. Sometimes, anyway."

"Come downstairs. I want you to hear the recording I made of the latest jam session. Rick and me primarily but we brought in Big Steve for background. I think we might have a sound."

Wayne deserved some attention. She was away all day and, for the past few months, had consistently had to bring work home. His music was his life.

"Give me five minutes to finish and I'll be down, okay? Time for you to put the kettle on?"

He looked at his watch. "I'll drag you down if it's more than five," he said.

She smiled. As Jade was frequently saying, as if. Wayne was a thin man with muscles that had never done more than hold up a guitar. But he had the most beautiful eyes she'd ever seen on a man. And a great smile. And, most of the time, he was easy to live with.

She was downstairs in four.

The music was more cacophony than harmony to her ears. But she knew she was ignorant of the finer details of composition and choreography of music. Or was it orchestration? Anyway, she nodded and smiled and smothered her yawns.

· · · · · ● · ● · · · ·

Ethan rang her at the office the next morning. "Nobody knows any Henry Macgregor at the charity shop you said he got the suit and tie from. But it's run by volunteers. You did say you'd found a volunteer who knew him?"

"Her name is Kathy. She's a middle-aged lady with a large nametag on her considerable bosom saying 'Kathy' with a 'K' and a 'y'." She spelled it out for him "Works Thursdays, for sure. And Fridays."

"My sergeant asked around at the shop. They didn't seem to know much about anything."

"Did he get the right charity shop?"

"Near the underpass?"

"That's the one. A hospice shop."

"He's now trying to find one Brody Somebody, a hot tip someone gave me. Given up on the second-hand shop."

"I'll pop over to the charity shop later today," she said with some alacrity. "I'd recognise her. I'll get her to come in and make a statement."

"Music to my ears," he said. "Now to Brody. Still no last name? The kids have clammed up, I suspect for the same reason young Brody is not coming in to talk to us."

"I'll ask my source," she said.

"You do that."

Maddie rang off and collected her bag. She didn't tell anyone where she was going, figuring she'd take her chances. It galled her that she'd even think of being compelled to tell someone when she left the office, something she'd felt no need to do in over a decade. And she was doubly irritated that this time she was going out on questionable probation business, and her guilt exacerbated her annoyance.

But the walk and fresh air cheered her up. Clouds alternated with sunshine enough to keep her encouraged. She could use more sunny weather.

She arrived at the charity shop to find it a hive of activity. She wandered around looking for Kathy, not finding her, and then waiting to ask one of the volunteers. In the meantime, she spotted the amber coloured necklace and held it up to the light. Either it was a very clever reproduction, or these beads were actually amber. No two beads were exactly alike and they were strung on a knotted thread, not something you often found nowadays, and never when the beads were plastic. The clasp was modern, but it could be a replacement. She fished out a two pound coin.

When she paid her money, she asked the young woman at the till if Kathy was working today.

"Hang on," she said and rushed over to an older woman. On her return, she said, "Kathy doesn't work here anymore. Sorry."

"Is the lady you spoke to the supervisor?"

At her nod, Maddie walked over to her and patiently waited until she was free. "I'm looking for Kathy who normally works here Thursdays and Fridays, maybe other days as well. I saw her last Friday and I know she was working on Thursday morning last week. I need to ask her something about that day."

"How do you know she worked that day?" the woman asked with a frown.

"She told me herself," Maddie said. ""

"Well, I'm afraid you're too late. She's gone."

"Gone? I don't understand."

"She's off to South Africa. She's always travelling. But I didn't hear about this trip until this week. And I've always thought of her as one of the sensible ones." She sighed heavily.

"I wonder if you could do me a favour," Maddie said. "I talked to an older lady last Friday, who knows Kathy. Could you please put me in touch with her?"

"Older? With white hair?"

"Lovely wavy white hair, yes."

"That would be Shirley. I could ask her."

A customer interrupted with a question and Maddie realised she'd get nothing more.

But she'd spotted a list of names and telephone numbers behind the desk when she was looking at the amber necklace. A quick reference list for contacting volunteers?

She waited for the young woman at the till to become distracted and left the till unattended. And waited some more. Finally, she realised her plan was not going anywhere. Not today anyway.

······●·●●···

After work, Maddie took out the amber beads and held them in her hands. Warm. Where had they come from? She fastened them around her throat, loving the look of them against her skin. Just the thing to wear under her open-necked white blouse.

Jade sloped in, sleeves too long, fringe hiding her eyes. Bored expression on her face. "What's for dinner?"

"Cold roast. Or I could heat it up in the leftover gravy. What do you fancy?"

"Pizza." Said without a smile.

"No pizza unless you're treating," Maddie said easily. "Beef in hot gravy or cold with horseradish."

"Not hungry." She opened the fridge and grabbed out some milk.

"How about a small portion? Which one?"

Jade sighed loudly. "Can't you just leave it, Mum? I'm not hungry." Meanwhile, she'd pulled the instant chocolate drink powder from the cupboard and was stirring a large spoonful into her milk.

"You need some protein, Jade. For true energy. How about a beef sandwich?"

Jade pulled out the bread.

Maddie figured that was a 'yes'.

"Any more on Brody?" she asked, without looking at her daughter.

"Nope. He's quit school though."

"When did that happen?"

"Dunno. Freya thinks it's all about that kid who died." Jade looked up, frowned at her mother's expression. "Don't go there, Mum."

Maddie continued to stare at her daughter, a chill spreading throughout her body.

"Don't you dare think what you're thinking," Jade said. "He's probably just upset. You know, grieving."

Chapter Eight

"Okay, we'll agree grieving is a real possibility," Maddie said. "But if he did quit school when Linsey Benton died, you can't blame me for thinking that could be significant. And the police will want to talk to him. Probably have already." But Jade had put earphones in and was eating her sandwich, her eyes on her phone.

Maddie sighed. Her older daughter Olivia had been an easy teen. Jade had shifted from being a bright little girl, social and enthusiastic, to this ... this Goth sitting in front of her ignoring her mother; it was as if a switch had been pulled one winter's day when she was fourteen. What should have been a few months, had been getting on for three very long years.

She sliced the beef and put it into the hot gravy while she dished up the potatoes and broccoli she'd been heating on the stove top. She set the table around Jade and called out to Wayne.

"Smells good," Jade said, emerging from whatever she'd been listening to. "Any extra?"

Maddie closed her eyes and took a deep breath. "There's enough for you. Any veggies to go with it?"

"No, just meat and gravy, thanks."

At least a 'thanks'.

"That girl who died, she was at school that morning, you know," Jade said.

"Was she?" Maddie murmured in a noncommittal response.

"Went off straight away, though. Freya says she was skiving school to meet up with Brody."

"Was she now...."

"Was who doing what?" Wayne asked, sitting himself down for dinner.

"That dead girl," Jade said. "She ran off that morning to meet up with her boyfriend."

He looked at Maddie.

She raised her eyebrows. Commenting would probably close Jade down.

"Freya heard he'd been at school that morning but only for an hour or two. Wagged the rest of the week. Now he's quit."

"Which school?" Wayne asked.

Jade shrugged. "One of the boys' schools in town. Kingston or Tiffins. Dunno." She looked up to see both parents looking at her. It was as if two were too many. She stood and slouched out after neatly arranging her knife and fork on her plate.

Maddie pointed to it after Jade was safely upstairs. "Gives me a particle of hope."

Wayne laughed.

After dinner, Maddie put a load of clothes into the washing machine. She'd asked Wayne to do it during the day, but, as so often happened, if she asked him to do something, he 'forgot'. If he thought of it himself, she had to make a fuss about what a good thing it was. So, it meant she was always having to make a decision whether to ask him to do something or wait until it intruded on his consciousness. And suffer whatever remained undone in silent frustration.

This boy Brody, surely the police would be closely questioning him. She knew, at the back of her mind, a new suspect, a better suspect, needed to be found to divert the police attention away from Henry. Could a new suspect be Brody? He sounded like a more likely option than Henry anyway.

But would that solve Henry's problem? Now he was in a proper prison again, things could stagnate. In circumstances like these, someone rotting in prison was out of mind, somehow. She'd known of many cases which ended up with apologies from the authorities when finally a wrongly accused, or even proven innocent person was released weeks, months even years afterwards. She was determined Henry would not be forgotten.

The phone rang.

"Madeleine? It's Sharon speaking."

Maddie hesitated for a split second. Then she knew. Aussie accent. Freya's mother.

"Hi. How are you?"

"Fine," she said in a distracted voice. "I … um, we have a great favour to ask. And if it is not convenient, just say the word. I know my Freya." She laughed.

Maddie laughed too, but more at Sharon's jumbled conversation than at Freya. Sharon was a sophisticated woman in high fashion, yet here she was stumbling over her words.

"Spit it out," Maddie said. "I'll react honestly."

"I have to be in New York next Friday. Big meeting. Flying me over. We thought maybe ...." She faltered again.

"Freya could stay here? Is that it?"

"Could she?" The relief came pouring down the line. "Donald and I thought we could make it a romantic weekend – long weekend – in New York for just the two of us. You know, marriages need a touch of romance every now and again." She was gabbling.

"No prob, Sharon. When are you leaving?"

"Thursday morning. We could see her off to school, then if she comes back to your place with Jade? We fly back Sunday afternoon."

Maddie did the arithmetic. Three nights including a school day and both days of the weekend. But teenagers don't need entertaining as such. Not these two Goths, anyway. "Have a lovely time, Sharon. And that idea of a weekend away does sound awfully enticing."

She came off the phone in a pensive mood. When had she and Wayne had a weekend away? Never? And having Freya now would mean Sharon and Donald owed them. Ideas started to whirl around her head. A weekend to rekindle romance. It felt like more than a good idea; it felt like a necessity.

· · · ● · ● · · · ·

On arrival at work the next day, she found a note on her desk saying she was to go to Romania's office as soon as she arrived. Maddie felt a fresh wave of frustration. This harassment was never ending. What had she done this time? Maybe taken longer than she was 'allowed' for her afternoon break when she went to the charity shop? She sighed and shoved her bag away before making a cup of tea and heading to Romania's office.

"Come in," she said to Maddie. "Sit."

Maddie bit back a retort that she was not a dog. Not even a bitch. The thought brought a smile to her lips.

"Nothing to smile about, Madeleine Brooks."

Maddie stared at her. The woman was beyond the pale. Who did she think she was, anyway? Treating professionals as if they were her own personal slaves. But Maddie was street-wise enough to keep her thoughts to herself.

"I gather you've been loading yet more work onto one of our Service Officers. I made a specific and totally clear directive to you that we are to lighten their load, not increase it. And you're not stupid; you understood. So, Ms Brooks, explain yourself."

Maddie looked at Romania and could only see an oversized Pitbull terrier. Slitty little eyes staring straight through her, growling, off the leash – all the signs she was after prey.

An overwhelming surge of frustration welled up and spilled over. "I'm giving you formal notice," Maddie said in a soft voice, "that as of right now, I plan on working to rule." She stood up and walked out. She was vaguely aware that Romania was talking, but the intense pounding in her ears meant she couldn't hear and she didn't stop. She grabbed her bag from her desk and continued walking until she was in the carpark and at her car. Her hands were shaking so hard, she couldn't work the remote key fob. She closed her eyes, breathed deeply and unclenched her hands, shoulders, jaw until finally the pounding lessened. She held her arms out. Still shaking, but not as much. She got the key into place and turned the car on. She drove the short distance to Starbucks and ordered a decaf coffee. She certainly didn't need caffeine when feeling like this. And she shouldn't be driving.

While drinking the coffee, letting her mind wander anywhere except work, she received a text.

Romania. She was suspended. HR would be in touch.

Chapter Nine

"What?" Wayne yelled. "What are you doing? You trying to bankrupt us right when I've been developing a new sound? And right when I need a new mixer to make it work? Your timing's just great. Bloody great."

"You're supposed to support me, not have a meltdown yourself," Maddie retorted. "Romania's impossible. If I have to quit, I have to. But it's not there yet, for heaven's sake. She's a child in an adult's clothing; she's having a temper tantrum."

"Dammit, woman, you're driving me crazy. Just pull your horns in, apologise. Hell, grovel, if you have to. Just make it right, okay?" With that, he stomped out of the kitchen leaving Maddie hunched over her mug of tea.

Her annoyance shrivelled, replaced with a feeling of ... of blah. Blah. No energy, no interest in doing anything, not wanting to eat, not wanting to drink her cooling tea, not wanting to move. She felt a tear trickling down one cheek. She let it fall from her face and watched it splash onto one hand resting on the kitchen table.

She sat there a long time.

After a disturbed night, the next morning Maddie dragged herself downstairs to make a phone call to Human Relations at work. She told the HR officer what had happened without emotion, as if giving a report on a client.

"There are procedures," the woman said calmly. "Your immediate boss – what is her name again?"

"Romania Carlisle. Kingston."

"Sorry, I'm not familiar with her."

"Newly appointed. And you'd better know that I was an unsuccessful applicant for that position."

A silence.

"Okay. Procedures," the woman continued. "You contact Carlisle's boss. She'll tell you to come in for an interview. And, a word to the wise, if you belong to the union, you should contact them straight away and put them in the picture." She paused again. "You are obviously a senior person without having anything like this in your past ... or I'd be familiar with your name. So, again, another word to the wise, write up a complete report ready for your boss's boss. Do you want me to look up who that is?"

"No need. She's Bettina Rossmoor. I know her."

"Do you know her personally?"

"Enough to nod to in the lift. That sort of thing."

"Start with the union."

Maddie thanked her and rang off.

A procedure. The big question: was the procedure written to redress the power differential, or to bolster a manager's power? In her present state of mind, she guessed it would be the latter.

Two cups of tea later, she rang the union. She'd paid her dues forever and never once had the occasion to ask for help until now. The thought churned her stomach.

The call was short. Neutral male voice, a low rumble. Maddie couldn't guess his age except not old. Contact Bettina Rossmoor. Make an appointment for next week. Let him know when. If he couldn't make the time agreed, she'd have to go back to Rossmoor for a new appointment. She was not, in any circumstances, to be persuaded to exclude the union. He was to be involved at all stages. Short and simple. But it relieved Maddie of a burden she didn't know she was carrying.

Might as well get on with it. She rang, had a short conversation with Rossmoor's secretary, made the appointment for Wednesday morning and rang the union rep with the time and date. All okay. Done.

She sat for a long moment, phone still in hand. Suddenly, she had nothing to do for several days. Its emptiness appalled her.

One more thing. Lawrence Reilly. She couldn't let him slip between the cracks again. She rang work, asked for Erin.

"Maddie. I've heard you've been suspended. Awful and so unfair. Are you okay?"

"A bit stunned, to tell the truth," Maddie said. "I left in such a hurry, I hadn't time to talk to you about Lawrence."

"Romania gave me the envelope. She was buzzing like an angry wasp, I can tell you, because she found some papers in your desk you hadn't told her about. I just said I knew about them and was expecting them."

"Thanks, Erin. Appreciate it." She told her about what had happened at the hospital.

"I gathered that. I rang the neurologist who sent his commiserations, by the way. Praised you to the heavens and wants to let your boss know. I said, write a letter."

"Not a bad time to get an appreciation letter, is it?"

"That's what I was thinking. Anyway, he has started Lawrence on some testosterone suppression medication to see if that helps."

"Fingers crossed," Maddie said.

After that, a cheese sandwich and a Granny Smith apple, she viewed life with a less jaundiced mind-set. She had things she wanted to do and now nobody to say she couldn't. It all came down to priorities. And sticking with her resolve of doing what she thought best.

Big Problem Number One: Henry, buried in prison.

And she was no longer his Probation Officer. And she knew nobody else would look after his back.

She needed to keep focussed. Reminded herself she now had the time for things she had only been able to accomplish around the demands of her job.

First priority for Big Problem Number One: get in touch with the elusive Kathy.

· · · · · · · · · ·

Maddie pretended to be interested in the revolving glass cabinet of jewellery where she'd first spotted her amber necklace. Not all that many people in the shop. Eventually, the woman behind the till, deep in a conversation, stepped away from the desk towards the person she was talking to. Instead of turning the cabinet, Maddie walked around it, as she'd done the week before until realising the cabinet revolved. Eyes firmly on a display of ancient watches, she hunkered down. Yes, the list she remembered was taped to the inner side wall of the desk. She spotted both the names 'Shirley' and 'Kathy'; both had telephone numbers attached. Both she committed to memory.

Maddie pretended to fumble her handbag, dropping it onto the floor with a clatter. She knelt down to reassemble it, grabbing her notepad and scribbling the two numbers down before standing up. Her memory was only so good.

Once outside the shop, she called Kathy's number. It rang then went into voice mail with Kathy's cheerful voice requesting a message. She dutifully left one requesting she got in touch with

DI de Roque to clarify Henry's purchase of the suit and tie on the day of his daughter's lunch; tell de Roque the time he was in the shop, if she remembered clearly.

The next phone number was for Shirley, and she recognised the voice immediately the call was answered. She explained how she needed to get in touch with Kathy. They had a cordial exchange of recalling the Friday when they'd met.

"Are you anywhere close to the charity shop, Shirley?"

"Five minutes away. Why?"

"I was just going to spoil myself with coffee and a muffin at the café opposite. Would you like to join me? My treat."

Soon the two of them were in easy chairs sitting in the bay window. Shirley, it turned out, was a fount of information.

"First, do you remember a man who bought a suit, shirt and tie on Thursday of last week? Thursday morning. Kathy helped him."

Shirley blew on the top of her coffee. "Not particularly. Any other clues?"

"He's middle height. Middle aged." She became aware of how generic Henry's outward appearance was. "Not fat, but certainly not slim. Slightly pudgy, I guess. Receding hairline. Hair going grey. A ready smile."

Shirley shook her head. "Describes half of our male customers." She took a delicate sip of her coffee. "Maybe not always the ready smile."

"No worries. He is rather generic looking, I guess. He was wearing dark trousers with a long sleeved dark green t-shirt under a zippered navy blue jacket. When he left, he was in the suit, shirt and tie he'd just purchased and the other clothes were left under the counter at the till. I picked them up for him on the Friday."

"I remember some clothes with a note pinned to them that they'd be picked up. Not the man, sorry."

"Okay, what about Kathy? The supervisor at the shop was surprised she'd gone on a trip without advance notice."

Shirley's eyes brightened. "I know. Amazing. Our Kathy does like her trips, but she's never gone as far as South Africa before. I can tell you one thing though, she's known forever she had an ancestor or two that went out there almost two hundred years ago. She's really excited to have the opportunity to fill in the missing bits in her genealogy charts."

"So, she's into genealogy."

"Chair of the Kingston chapter. Has been for ages. Only last week she gave us a lecture about what to do when gaps are found in the records and what can be done about it. Mentioned the South African connection; that's why I know about it. Are you interested in tracking your ancestors?"

Maddie smiled. "I guess everyone wonders where they've come from. But I have no knowledge beyond my great-grandparents. Maybe some day. It sounds like a fun hobby."

"You'll have to join our society. I'm always getting really good hints from other members."

Where had she heard about the Genealogy Society before? Yes, of course. It was Henry. He'd planned on joining.

"Back to Kathy," Maddie said. "She suddenly found some missing ancestors in South Africa?"

"Not suddenly. But she had some ideas for tracking them down which she shared with us at our last meeting. Someone at the meeting offered her the opportunity to carry it through."

"How?"

"A few days later, she got a call from a distant cousin she didn't know she had. From South Africa, visiting his daughter here in London, trying to persuade the young woman to go home, but, I gather the daughter wasn't having any. The fellow heard Kathy's talk and contacted her. His name is Milhousen. Like Kathy's but with an extra 'n' at the end. Said his daughter wasn't going to use the ticket back to South Africa he'd already bought. If Kathy wanted it, it was hers."

"What marvellous luck," Maddie said with genuine enthusiasm.

"She'd be on her own there, as Mr Milhousen was staying in London to see if he could put some more pressure on the daughter. Something about the daughter and an unsuitable young man. The usual story."

"Kathy took advantage of the offer?"

"And how! She took only a couple of hours to pack, madly ringing around cancelling stuff. Getting me to look after her cat. Excited as a child going to the circus for the first time. She said this was a massive opportunity to complete her genealogy searches, funded by a distant relative she didn't even know from South Africa."

"Amazing." Maddie sat back, staring out the window at the passing foot traffic. On reflection, just a bit too amazing, somehow, but that was her cynical nature coming out, honed by too many years as a Probation Officer. Or was it just her dark mood returning? "Tell me a bit about her. Does she do this sort of thing often?"

"Someone gives her a free plane ticket? Hardly. She's a retired kindergarten teacher. Lived at home looking after her elderly mother for far too long. Then inherited the house, sold it, moved into a flat near me and quit her job. She's been living quietly ever since – punctuated by trips all over the country – and enjoying every minute of searching for ancestors and distant cousins. She's a real enthusiast. Loves talking about it to everybody she meets." Shirley finished the last of her muffin and dabbed at her lips carefully with the paper serviette.

Maddie sat silently going over the story. A wonderful opportunity for Kathy, for sure. She sighed. "Back to my problem. Are there any records that will show someone purchased a man's suit last week on Thursday?"

Shirley shook her head. "No. We just record the money we take in. No details. Sorry."

"Can you remember which day you saw the clothes with the note?"

"Let's see. Thursday or Friday, I guess."

They parted with thanks each to the other and genuine smiles.

Once walking back to her car Maddie asked herself, just who is this Milhousen character who has money to spare that he gifts a flight to South Africa to someone he's just met?

Once home, Maddie found herself staring at her cell phone. She sighed and picked it up. Put it down. Came to a decision. She positioned the cell phone against her mug and took a photo. A small adjustment, another photo. Yes. She grabbed her landline and dialled Romania, reached over to the cell phone and started a video recording. Of course, it wouldn't record Romania but it would record her own words and, maybe importantly – who knew? – her facial expressions. All perfectly legal.

"Romania?" she asked, then identified herself.

"How dare you!" The words were spat into the phone.

"How dare I what?" Maddie asked, non-plussed.

"Going above my head. You are a sneaky, manipulative, calculating schemer, Madeleine Brooks. No wonder they wanted me, not you, in this position."

"I'm sorry you find me sneaky and manipulative. And a calculating schemer, Romania. You told me to contact HR. I did contact them. They advised me on the proper protocol. Check with them."

"You went above my head!" Her voice had risen in both tone and volume.

"My seeing your boss *is* the protocol. Nothing to do with me. I only went above your head, as you put it, because I was told to.

By HR." She took a deep breath. "But it doesn't have to come to this…."

"You have no idea the consequences of your actions. And if you think you'll get away scot free, you have another think coming."

"How about we meet somewhere neutral? Over a drink, perhaps, and we can…."

"No bloody way will you get me…." The phone went blank.

Romania had rung off.

Maddie took another deep breath. "We're both professionals, Romania," she said into the empty phone. "We are adult women, highly educated in our chosen profession, successful, even, but with a difference of opinion. I've dealt with Service Officers for years and I'm sure you have too." She let a small pause stretch for a count of three. "I know. Perhaps part of the problem is I've had only one boss since I started here in Kingston almost twenty years ago. We undoubtedly developed a certain way of handling problems here. But nothing is set in stone. If we – the two of us – can just sit down…." She paused again, letting a frown crease her forehead. "Romania? Are you there? Romania?" She lowered the phone and pressed the red end button and looked at the cell phone recording her face and actions. "She rang off." She paused, looking down at the landline receiver before reaching over and turning off the recording.

She played it back. Nothing but the occasional unintelligible squawk from Romania's end. And the last bit took an additional 21 seconds only. That should be okay. She saved it onto her laptop and again onto a memory stick which she threw behind the insert in her cutlery drawer. Just in case.

Funny how predictable people can be when in the grip of emotion. For the first time in weeks, she felt a surge of confidence.

Chapter Ten

Jade sighed heavily. Her mother could be so unimaginative at times. So by-the-book. It really surprised her to find she was threatening to quit her job. And Dad was being a prick. As usual.

They were in the kitchen, each making their own breakfast. She'd poured herself some Coco Pops, as few as possible, but enough to avoid yet another argument when she didn't want to eat before school.

"What's up today?" her mother asked.

Jade shrugged. "The usual."

"Have you thought of anything more about Brody ... what was his last name again?"

Jade knew full well she'd never given her mother Brody's last name. "Nothing," she said. She noticed her mother's strained face and her heart relented. "I can ask around," she said.

"That would be...." Her mother stopped. Shook her head. "Actually, maybe it's best you let sleeping dogs."

"Don't fuss, Mum. I'm not going to talk to anybody but my own friends, okay?"

Her mother frowned. "Still, word can get out. And we're talking about a murder. No, I think we'd better forget I brought it up."

Jade left for school determined she would not let it go. For heaven's sake, nobody could find out anything other than someone at school. The kids had all gone onto protection mode about Brody. But what if he really had murdered Linsey?

The opportunity came at morning break when Freya told Kim and some of their other friends that Brody had wagged school since Linsey died and had now left. He was working mowing lawns with his older brother.

"I'm not sure about him," Kim said. "He can be dangerous."

The other girls turned towards her. Kim was quiet. A pretty girl but small and studious. Jade had always liked her. They'd known each other for years. Still going to their school even though Kim and her family now lived outside of Esher somewhere.

"Yeah?" Jade said. "What kind of dangerous?"

"When he's drinking, he can be … you know." Her voice faded and she looked down.

"Sex?" Jade asked. "Did he come onto you?"

Kim blushed. "Yes. No. Actually teasing. That's what it was. Teasing."

"Come on, Kim. Out with it," Freya said.

Jade had always thought Freya was just a little jealous that Kim and Jade had been friends forever.

Kim's colour deepened. "Maybe it was nothing. I don't know… but it makes me sick to the stomach thinking about it, that's all."

"Better out than in," Jade said, immensely curious that something had happened to Kim that she had not discussed with her in private. "If you want, that is. Only if you want to, Kim."

Kim looked at Jade. "You remember that party we went to in Oxshott woods?"

Jade nodded. Last summer. They were supposed to be at the flicks but instead piled into a couple of cars and headed out of town. Accompanying them were several large bottles of homebrewed beer one of the boys had discovered in his attic. Years old and it tasted like it, but lots of people drank it anyway. Sick to her stomach? Probably that awful beer.

"He dropped his trou. His friends were all shouting and egging him on. His thing was all … big and red. He shoved it into my face."

"Yetch," Freya said. "What did you do?"

"Smacked it away," she said. "Hit it, actually, with my fist. Didn't want to touch it with my fingers."

"Should have punched him in the goolies," one of the other girls said.

"Hitting his willy would've done the job," Jade said loyally. She burst into laughter. "Good on you, Kim! God, I'd love to have seen it!"

"Oh, for a selfie of that!" shouted Freya. "Good one, Kim."

"I sure wish you guys had been there then," she said with a growing smile.

"I bet it hurt like crazy," Jade said with delight. "And I'm not talking about his silly willy. I'm talking about where it really hurts – his ego!"

They trouped back to class with smiles all around. But it set Jade to thinking along a different track. This guy was no longer the poor picked upon, grieving guy she'd thought. She'd need to know more. And she would learn more. Oldies couldn't do it. But she could.

After school she ran straight home. After changing into jeans and a discarded black pullover of her father's, she opened the garden shed to drag out her bike, the layer of dust showing how she'd ignored it for the last year or so. She pedalled off, traversing up and down each street methodically but quickly, searching for any sign of freshly mown grass. She knew the old guy who mowed their neighbour's lawns had territories. He spent the day in separate smallish areas. Fingers crossed Brody's brother used the same technique.

Half an hour later, the smell of mown grass alerted her. She spotted an open van full of gardening tools parked in front of a large house set on a double lot. She got off her bike and walked on the footpath pushing the bike alongside of her. Sure enough, she soon heard sounds of a lawn mower. Do gardeners work normal hours? It was almost five. She stopped several metres past the van and turned her bike upside down. And quietly let some of the air out of her front tyre.

She didn't have to wait long.

"Problems?"

She was standing with one hand squeezing the tyre, looking into the middle distance. She whirled around. "Oops, sorry. Startled me."

"Puncture?" The young man looked enough like Brody to be his brother, as long as Brody hadn't made big changes since they'd met at the forest party some months before.

"I suppose so. I haven't been on my bike for yonks. Maybe just a slow leak?"

Brody came from around the side of the house pushing a lawn mower. "What's up?" He and his brother were both tall with wavy dark hair and sleepy grey eyes. The brother was heavier, most likely because he'd been doing a physical job for some time. They were obviously brothers.

"Oh, hi, Brody. I didn't know you were working now. Mowing, I see."

He frowned. "Yeah. Gardening. For now, anyway." He stared at her. "I know you. Can't remember your name. Friend of Freya's, right?"

"That's me. Jade. Remember?" She turned to the bike. "Got a slow leak here. I think, anyway."

"Get the mower in the back, bro," the brother said. "Then pull the red bag out from under the bench. Should be a foot pump in there."

"You're Brody's brother, then?" Jade asked him.

"For my sins," the young man said. He turned away and yelled, "Find it, Bro?"

"Yeah. You get on with things. I'll do it," Brody said, emerging from the van with a large red sports bag. He knelt by the bike while his brother occupied himself placing gardening tools into the back of the van.

"Thanks, Brody," Jade said. "Hey, look, I'm sorry about Linsey."

He shook his head. "Bad." He connected the screw fitting onto the tyre and started pumping. "I'll do the other tyre now we're at it," he said.

When he finished, Jade and Brody righted the bike. "I appreciate it, thanks." She was flummoxed on how to continue the conversation.

"You going to Alfie's bash on Saturday?" He looked straight into her eyes.

She'd heard about the party. Usually she paid little attention to the more wild sounding social activities open to most and she had intended ignoring this one. Still.... "Yeah, thought I'd go. For a while at least."

"See you there, then, okay?"

She smiled at him. "Okay." Code for a half promise they'd look out for each other.

Maybe.

· · · ● ● ● ● ● · · ·

Saturday morning, Jade had to wait for Freya to wake up. It was fun having her over, but there was something to be said for having her bedroom to herself. She wondered how Kim survived having to share with her little sister. She and Olivia had always had their own bedrooms. As soon as Olivia got married, her old bedroom was turned into her mum's home office.

Jade heard noises in the kitchen. She quietly slipped out of her room and headed downstairs.

"Morning," her mother said. "What are you two up to this weekend?"

"The flicks tonight. Might have a bite afterwards."

"Home by the last bus, please, Jade. Everything by the board this weekend."

Jade knew that was because Donald and Sharon were unseen presences. She nodded. "Yeah, whatever."

"Studying?"

"I know. I have only two exams to go, thank goodness. I can get a bit done after Freya leaves on Sunday," Jade said. "We're going to do some English together today. And I'm about to start my swot for history tomorrow. Should have been last week."

"And you haven't started it yet? Jade!"

"I know. I wish I was more interested in the medieval period. Stupid – I thought it would be all about lords and their battles, and ladies and their castles, not stupid politics."

"I have an ancestor who came over with William the Conqueror," a voice said from the hallway. "Dad knows all about stuff like that," Freya said as she sat at the kitchen table. "He's always banging on about the Dymock family tree. He can tell you all sorts of stories from way back. You should ask him for some stuff you can throw in."

"Too late at this point." Jade smiled at Freya. "But it does sound interesting."

"Yeah. Whatever. Everything becomes boring by the time it's part of the school curriculum."

"I should have chosen the Victorian era," Jade said. She turned to her mother who was pouring mugs of tea for the two girls. "Remember Princess Victoria when she was a child and going to church in Esher? The old church?"

Victoria, as a child, spent a lot of time at Claremont with her mother and her favourite uncle. Claremont, the most famous house in their general vicinity. And it was only a few miles from where they lived in Surbiton. She loved Claremont. The Brooks family had often motored out there for picnics and countryside walks when the girls were small. They'd heard many anecdotes over the years and probably, she figured, that was the origin of her interest in history.

"Remember the story about Victoria sitting up on the special royal balcony at the old church in Esher and getting too close to a burning brazier?" she asked her mother.

"Of course," Maddie said, joining in Jade's enthusiasm. "It was designed to shield the royals from the winter cold," she said to Freya. "Nobody else had heating in the freezing church, of course. Have you been there?"

Freya, busy with a bite of toast, shook her head.

Jade enthused about Claremont to Freya while they ate.

"I'm not sure why you didn't choose that era for your A Levels," her mother said.

Jade looked up, annoyed. "I just didn't, all right? But it's not relevant now. So let's forget it. I've got to concentrate on the stupid twelfth century." She glared at her mother then remembered how things weren't going very well in her life. "I mean thanks, Mum, for reminding me of why I love history. And I mean thanks. Now it's my job to make something of this stupid exam, yeah?"

Her mother smiled. "So much more to choose from next year. You'll get your enthusiasm back, I bet. I certainly did when I started uni."

"It's what keeps me going. But don't remind me of anything but the twelfth century, for the next little while, okay?"

"Got it," Maddie said.

• • • •• •• • • ••

"You ready yet?" Freya said as she completed her face with black lipstick. "Hurry up. We're going to be kicked out."

The girls had dawdled in the John Lewis loos, putting on the layers of makeup a true Goth needed to obliterate all signs of freckles or natural colouring. But the shops were closing and it was almost late enough to go to the party. Not that they could stay long. Back by midnight, Jade's mother had insisted, in spite of pleas to the contrary. She thought they were going to the flicks then out for a sweet afterwards.

The plan was to split up when they got to Alfie's and meet again outside the front door of the house at eleven-thirty so they could catch the last bus home together. Plans made well ahead of time knowing how noisy it would be once they got there.

The music from the party was audible as soon as they turned into the street. Once inside, the noise was deafening. Before heading towards the kitchen, Jade waved at Freya who gave her a thumb's up. A lot of guys hung out in the kitchen, in her not-so-vast experience. Freya had disappeared into the lounge in search of someone – anyone – interesting.

It was crowded and it seemed everybody was taller than her. She finally made it to the kitchen bench where someone asked if she wanted a beer. She nodded and was handed a bottle. She pretended to take a long swallow. She planned on making this beer last her the whole time of the party. She needed all her wits to cope with a maybe-murderer.

Time dragged. She pretended to drink, occasionally greeting people she knew, listening into several conversations and wishing she were elsewhere.

"Jade. You're here." Brody, speaking directly into one ear, gave her shoulders a quick squeeze.

She turned to him with a smile. "They have a garden?" she asked.

He nodded and grabbed the hand not occupied with the beer and elbowed his way outside dragging Jade behind him.

"Better?" he asked once outside.

"At least I can hear you," she said. She looked at the scene before her. "Nice place."

It was. Fairy lights had been strung along bushes behind a grand swimming pool. Wide steps led down from a narrow deck. The noise of music and people yelling at each other faded as someone closed the back door. It was cool, but almost pleasant after the overcrowding inside the house. Brody sank down on the top step and patted the spot beside him. Jade joined him. So far, so good.

"Looks as if you're back in the social merry-go-round," Jade said with some hesitation. It was all she could think of to say to turn the conversation to where she wanted it to go. She needed to avoid anything that could lead to the sort of situation Kim had faced.

"Yeah, I guess," he said.

"You really cared for Linsey."

He shrugged. "I didn't know she was only thirteen. She said she was sixteen."

"She could have been," Jade said. It was hardly the truth. Linsey was small and young looking. She hadn't been surprised she was only thirteen.

Brody was silent. He made a slight noise and Jade looked across at him.

He was crying.

"Oh, Brody," she whispered, her heart lurching. This wasn't fun anymore. This was real. She put her hand on his forearm.

He shook her off. Stood up, facing down the garden. "Tell the truth, we didn't have that much in common," he said in a strange voice. "You know. She was into boy bands in a big way. She's caused me trouble. Big trouble."

Jade noted the sudden change of direction. Safer subject for him, she was sure.

"The police?"

"They'll want to question me, for sure. Linsey was sort of my girlfriend even though I was breaking up with her. Always crying to get her own way. She was bloody thirteen. I shoulda known."

"Yeah, that's trouble," Jade said softly.

He sighed. "And she's dead." He gulped. "I didn't do it, you know." He flopped back down beside Jade and pulled his knees up to his chin. "I never forced her to do anything. She was willing. More than."

Jade realised with a start that he was talking about sex, not the murder.

He laughed. "Bloody begging for it. Can hardly tell that to the cops, though, could I."

Jade kept silent, following him without difficulty. "The thirteen stuff. Okay."

"I'll have to tell them it was all innocent." He shook his head. "As if."

"Maybe she was willing to … um … you know, with some other guys."

He whirled on her and Jade cowered back. "Sorry, Brody. Sorry. Just a thought, okay?"

He slumped back. "She wasn't a virgin, yeah? So, okay, somebody else had been there." He shook his head violently. "Drop it, okay?"

Not a particularly useful bit of information. Like, it wasn't as if anybody would come forward to admit having had sex with a thirteen year old, especially when she'd turned up dead in the Thames. Jade took a swig of her beer. A proper swig this time. She wanted to look at the time but didn't dare interrupt what was going on.

"Look, she has … no, I mean, she had this arsehole of a stepfather. A right minger, okay?"

Jade stared at him. What was he saying? "She told you…? She did it with her father?"

He stared back at her. "Step." He reached over her arm for her beer. "Can I have some?"

"Sure." Jade hated saying so; she was squeamish about other people's saliva. Knew it was the last time she'd put that bottle to her own lips. Ick. "It's all yours. I've had enough."

He tipped the bottle back and drank deeply.

Jade stole a quick glance at her phone. Time to wrap this up. She stood and stretched. "Look, any time you want to talk, just call, okay?"

He looked up at her, surprise showing on his face. "Hey, thanks. I think I've turned the corner now, but thanks, anyway."

She touched him lightly on the shoulder and headed down the steps so she could walk around the house to the front without having to elbow her way through the crowd inside.

"You meeting Freya?"

"Yeah. Outside at the front."

"I'll walk you there."

Freya was already waiting. She frowned as she saw who was with Jade.

"Thanks, Brody. See you later," Jade said to accentuate their parting.

On the bus, Freya turned to Jade. "Why were you with that eejit?"

"Getting info for my mother. But don't you say anything. I have to handle this very carefully, yeah?"

Freya gave her a quick smile. "Don't worry. I get it."

Chapter Eleven

Sunday, unlike on previous weekends, was just another day for Maddie now that the huge contrast in stress levels between weekdays and weekends had been smoothed. After a leisurely shower she wandered down to breakfast close to nine o'clock. Plenty of time before cooking Sunday lunch. Olivia, son-in-law Brian and the grandchildren were coming, which made, including Freya, eight at the table.

Weekends were usually busy for Wayne, as all the other members of his group worked at day jobs and were only free to be at the studio weekends. Given the dirty crockery still on the table Maddie knew he'd breakfasted on cereal and toast and was long gone off to his shared studio.

No sign of the girls. Freya's parents said they'd be returning Sunday afternoon. Maybe Freya would be there for Sunday lunch, maybe not. Maddie was cooking a large joint, which should be enough for several dinners through the coming week even with eight to feed today.

Freya had been an easy guest. The girls were at an age when constraints probably should be lifted, but Maddie found it difficult. Jade was young for her age, as was Freya. And she didn't trust them to make sensible decisions. Even as the thoughts were passing through her head, she realised she was being over-protective. She also felt the usual burden of having another child in the house under her care.

She rang her older daughter.

"Hi Olivia," she asked. "All okay for Sunday lunch?"

"Absolutely. See you later," Olivia said. "I'm just off to take Robbie to his baby swimming lesson."

"So you did decide to enrol him, after all."

Olivia prattled on about what a good idea it was, the safety aspects of teaching a child early on how to swim and then rang off when she realised the time. Maddie came from the phone call reassured life was progressing as it should in some parts of her world, at least.

An hour or so later, the two teenaged girls appeared in the kitchen, eyes still heavy with sleep. As they grabbed breakfast food, Maddie asked them about the film they'd seen the night before.

"Not so great," Jade said. "But we got ice cream sundaes afterwards. Worth the evening out, weren't they, Freya?"

"Yeah, great," she said, her eyes on the cereal she was eating.

Maddie inwardly sighed. So, they didn't go to the flicks. But they did come home on time as she well knew. No harm done. But she'd have to figure out a way to indicate they didn't have to lie. Somehow.

"I gather you know this Brody fellow," she said to Freya. "What do you think of him?"

"Not much," Freya said with a quick glance at Jade. "Not my type."

"He's not so bad," Jade said. "I like tall boys. And he has nice eyes."

Maddie frowned. Jade was vulnerable. She'd had a romance during the winter, which, when it broke apart, had left her silent and more stroppy than usual for several weeks. First loves. Always a problem. But a short problem. Jade was now back to her usual awkward Goth-type self.

"He's working now. In his brother's gardening business." Jade kept her head down, concentrating on slicing cheese for a grilled sandwich. "I think he's over Linsey. We saw him in town last night, didn't we, Freya."

"You talked to him, not me," she muttered.

"Jade, I told you…." Maddie glared at her daughter.

"Hold on, Mum. If I'd been rude to him, that would have alerted him that something was up, okay? I chatted to him and now you've got something you can follow up." She shoved her sandwich under the grill. "Man, I can't do anything right around here."

Maddie inwardly rolled her eyes. Teenagers. She straightened and lightened her tone. "You're absolutely right. An easy chat is exactly what was appropriate given Freya knows the boy."

"And is it important you know where he's working?"

"I imagine it's very important."

Maddie went upstairs to collect washing from the bedrooms. At the top of the stairs, she realised she could hear the girls talking in the kitchen. Talking about somebody. Still discussing Brody? She paused.

"Do you believe him?" Freya asked.

"Why would he lie about it?" Jade's voice was scornful.

"Because people lie about sex all the time, that's why."

"Yeah. Okay. But her stepfather? That's beyond gross."

Maddie took a deep breath. Stepfather? The only stepfather in the picture was Linsey Benton's.

"Sort of makes it more real," Freya said. "Because nobody, like *nobody*, would make up a story about having sex with a total munter like him."

"Ugly. Old. And sort of a father. Way past yuck."

· · • • • · • • • ·

Later, the girls went off for a swim – in a rainstorm – in the heated outdoor pool in Hampton on the edge of Bushy Park. Once alone, Maddie searched the local equivalent of the yellow pages and found three gardening firms advertising their services. Old Mr McGurk's small advertisement was there plus 'Kingston Gardening Services, est. 1993' and 'Frederickson Lawns and Gardens'. She hesitated about ringing Ethan on a Sunday. Tomorrow would do. She concentrated on cleaning up the kitchen as she put on the roast and vegetables. They could have ice cream for a sweet. Easy.

Olivia and her family arrived in time and the girls followed shortly. Maddie looked at her watch. No sign of Wayne. She briefly considered texting him that everyone was already there, but dismissed the thought. He'd only rant about her smothering him. One of his favourite complaints over the years.

She had just called everyone to the table when the doorbell rang.

"I'll get it," yelled Olivia's older child, Bonita, who saw herself as a four-year-old society hostess.

"Come on in," she said loudly at the front door. "We're going to have Sunday lunch. You can have some too. We have loads."

The Dymocks came in with apologies for their awkward timing but Maddie insisted Bonita was right – they had a big Sunday lunch with plenty for two more. After a bit of social fiddle-faddle, Donald and Sharon joined the overflowing table.

As she was clearing the lunch things from the table before bringing out the sweet, Wayne sauntered in with charming – to the others, at least – apologies. Ice cream was served with a spoonful or two of Drambuie for the adults and chocolate sauce for the children including an unprotesting Freya and a protesting Jade. The meal became even noisier than before with children's squeals dominating, egged on by the teenagers. Still, Wayne managed to hold forth about his new sound to Donald and Brian while Maddie, Olivia and Sharon had a constantly interrupted conversation about New York. By three-thirty, Freya and her parents had left, with an invitation to their house next weekend for an 'Aussie Barbie'.

A barbecue at the Dymocks. Nice to be invited. Very nice.

Chapter Twelve

Monday dawned with Wayne going back to the studio to clean up after their weekend's work, slightly surprising, but pleasing nonetheless. Maddie knew fast food containers would litter the place, ashtrays would be full and paper would be strewn everywhere as the musicians wrote down ideas, abandoned them and wrote more. Although years before Wayne had asked Maddie to clean up there, she'd refused as part of her acknowledgment the studio was his space. Also, given Wayne was loath to do any housework at home, fair's fair.

She was just emptying the dishwasher from the clean-up after the Sunday lunch when her telephone rang. Ethan.

"We picked up the boyfriend yesterday."

Maddie felt relieved he'd found the lad without her grassing on him. "How did you find out where he was?"

"A little birdie. A man, actually, voice heavily disguised. Said the lad was working for his brother as a gardener."

Maddie was startled. Exactly the same information she would have given Ethan if she'd called. "Anything come from it?"

"He was questioned for several hours; the lads will be checking his story. We've let him go but he's still a person of interest."

"Four hours on a Sunday? That's dedication to duty."

"It was important. Damn those kids hiding him from us."

"Yeah. Well, if you lived with a teenager, you wouldn't be surprised. Better get used to not knowing what your kids are up to."

"I'll bribe them. No television before they spill all."

"Television? You must be kidding," Maddie said. "Hey, what can I do for you this fine Monday morning?"

"Just warning you I'm dropping in. Have the kettle on."

"Will do."

"See you in ten."

It was only after clicking off she realised he knew she was not at work.

· · · ● ● ● ● · · ·

"How did you hear about my little problem with work?" she asked him as she ushered him into the living room.

"Some young lady from your office who looked barely out of her teens. She said someone else had taken over Henry Macgregor's case. Seems she's a junior Service Officer for the Probation Service. That means she's an underling, right?"

"Right." Maddie was busy pouring boiling water over teabags in the kitchen. "Did you get her name?"

"Something old fashioned. Agatha Somebody?"

"She's young but bright," Maddie said as she brought the mugs into the sitting room. "Maybe the best of the bunch. So she's taking over Henry?"

"No. She had come to talk over one of her cases, not Macgregor, but she was told to inform me about another Probation Officer taking over Macgregor's management. Her boss. Romania Somebody? Isn't that the new supervisor who's causing you grief?"

Maddie was stunned. So stunned, she just stared at Ethan.

"Bad news, presumably," he said lightly. He sipped his too hot tea and put it down on the coffee table. "Spill all, Maddie. What's going on?"

She brought him up to date with her problems with Romania.

He shook his head. "Someone of your stature and experience, that's more than stupid," he said. "Give the boss's boss my name. Tell him we've been working together for a decade or more."

"Her. Actually, it's been thirteen years," she said with a smile. "And thanks, I will. And I'd do the same if you had this sort of problem."

He waved that suggestion away and changed the subject. "Brody Frederickson. Your daughter knows him. Maybe I could have a quiet word with her."

Maddie sat still for a moment, pondering the pros and cons. "Probably not at the moment. She's in the middle of her A Level exams. I can tell you she does know Frederickson, but only recently. She's feeling sympathetic and protective."

"Thought you'd say that." He grabbed a digestive biscuit from the plate Maddie had brought out. "So far, he's checking out, but we're waiting for his shoes to be compared to some footprints we found at the scene."

She needed to find a natural opening. "What are you going to do about the underage sex bit?"

"Let him sweat." He paused. "For a while anyway." He grinned, then it faded. Some of my guys are quite keen on young Frederickson for our perp. It does take some of the heat off Henry Macgregor, I suppose."

Maddie looked at him keenly. "You're not happy with either, are you?"

"Early days."

"Not really, Ethan."

"Stand corrected. Not so early days, which is why my guys are so interested in Frederickson."

"Can we get Henry released?"

He shook his head slowly. "They are showing interest in Frederickson, maybe, but Macgregor is still *numero uno*, Maddie. Sorry."

They sat drinking their tea, rain making rivulets down the front windows.

"I gather Frederickson says he never met Linsey's family," Maddie said.

"So the girl didn't want him to meet them," Ethan said. "I guess we know why."

"Of course."

Maddie paused. "I noticed when the parents were interviewed on telly, the stepfather was irate." She spoke softly. "Over the top. Strange guy. And I have something I want to tell you about him."

"Something other than expressing his anger at her murder? A displacement?" They both knew this was a frequent occurrence.

"Something the boy said. Brody. Something he told … told Jade. Maybe Jade and her friend. I overheard a discussion between the two of them."

Ethan straightened. Looked straight into her eyes. "Go on…."

"Apparently Linsey told Brody she'd been sexually abused by her stepfather." Too often, in Maddie's experience, sexual abuse reared its ugly head and complicated the picture.

"Okaaay." He drew out the word. "Did he say more? Any details we can use?"

"Just that Linsey was needy. Brody wanted to break off with her. She threw herself at him."

"He's not claiming he didn't have a sexual relationship with her?"

Maddie sorted out the double negative and gave him a sad smile. "Sorry. Not the type of subject my contact would discuss with me."

He smiled, stretching out his long arms. "Frederickson will come round to admitting it. I can see the signs. At the moment he's claiming it was just platonic. And he's not said a word to us about the stepfather."

"What about the mother? Is she strange too?" Maddie brought to mind the weeping woman from the television interview.

"The mother just shook her head when told about the boyfriend. Presumably in disappointment. Didn't glance at the stepfather."

She smiled sadly. "And, of course, we don't know that Linsey and Brady did have sex."

Ethan shrugged. "The coroner said 'recent sexual activity' but not immediately before death."

"Could be yet another boyfriend?"

"That's getting farfetched. Probably she was with Frederickson a day or so earlier. Of course, it might have been the stepfather." He shook his head. "Complications."

"I hate to think of a little girl like that in a sexual relationship with anybody. Losing her childhood." Maddie finished her tea with a sigh. "So I take it Brody Frederickson has not been arrested. Damn. I'd hoped he would be of sufficient interest that Henry could be released."

Ethan shook his head. "Doesn't work that way. You know that."

"I can hope." She smiled.

Ethan smiled back, finished his tea and rose. "Let me know anything more you hear about young Frederickson." He sat back down. "Sorry, Maddie, I've been so focussed on him, I didn't ask you about what the next steps will be in your work situation."

Maddie filled him in, pulling no punches. "I've got the union watching my back. Thank goodness for small mercies. Maybe I can even keep my job."

"I'd hate to lose you," he said as he again arose. "Keep in touch. And let me know if there's any other way I can contribute."

•••••••••••

After school, Jade's phone rang when she was half way home. "You doing anything?" Brody's voice.

"On my way home. Why, what's up?"

"Nothing." He paused. "Well, something. I just got out of the police station."

"No," Jade said.

"Hours and bloody hours of questions – yesterday and again today."

"But they let you go, right?"

"Yeah. For now." He took a deep, audible breath. "They took my Nikes. Bloody pigs."

"You can see why, Brody. Besides, maybe it'll be your shoes that'll prove your innocence."

He took a deep shuddering breath. "Yeah. Yeah, you're right. Hadn't thought of it that way. If they have footprints, they won't be mine." He paused again. "Don't trust them, though."

"Can I do anything?"

"Nah. But it's good talking to you. Never thought about how my shoes could actually help. Hey, thanks for that."

"Any time," Jade said. As a pause deepened, she said, "Bye, Brody. Keep smiling, yeah?" She tucked her phone away, feeling distinctly uncomfortable about her role in Brody's distress. Her bloody mother had rung her bloody cop friend. So much for discretion. It seemed it only went one way.

Chapter Thirteen

Maddie took advantage of a mild sunny day to get into the garden and do some much needed weeding. She had always done her most constructive thinking while her hands were busy – often in the kitchen or hanging out laundry, but weeding was high on the list as well. She drew on her gardening gloves, moved her kneeler into position and started pulling. What were weeds anyway? Just successful plants growing in the wrong place. She had a sneaking affection for them and merely wished they hadn't settled in her garden rather than some bit of neglected land elsewhere.

She'd had a short conversation with Jade over breakfast, or what Jade liked to think was breakfast. Brody was complaining he had to give up his trainers for analysis. That was interesting. The only reason the police would want his trainers would be if they had a footprint, a partial one, at least.

"Maybe it's not such a good idea to have much to do with Brody right now," she suggested, keeping her eyes away from her daughter's.

"I don't have 'much to do' with him." She mimed the quotation marks.

"The police are questioning him. Isn't that enough?"

"Leave it," Wayne said to Maddie. "Jade is old enough to pick and choose her own friends."

"I know," Maddie acknowledged, reluctant to have a row with him. "Sorry, Jade. Just being my usual over-protective self."

She flashed her mother a half smile and used the opportunity to leave the kitchen, with most of her cereal uneaten.

"Glad you listened to me for once," Wayne said.

Maddie bit back a reply. She hated, hated it when Wayne rubbed it in.

Instead she turned her back on her husband and her thoughts to Henry's clothes. He favoured rather upmarket Ecco casual shoes; they'd had a discussion about them one day. Henry owned two pairs, apparently carefully preserved from before his incarceration, one pair dark brown and the other black and lovingly polished whenever Maddie noticed them, presumably to prolong their useful lives. The parcel of clothes she'd picked up from the day of Linsey's murder contained no shoes. Ergo, either Henry wore his usual Eccos both to the charity shop and away from it now decked out in his new suit – would he do that? – the black pair would be marginally all right to wear with a suit, or he'd rid himself of incriminating trainers at the charity shop when he bought the outfit for his daughter's lunch. It would have been possible. Just slip them in amongst the shoes for sale. But he'd have to buy shoes to wear with the suit. Nobody had mentioned shoes at all. Besides, she'd never seen him in trainers.

Brody, of course, did own at least one pair of trainers. But he was released after questioning by the police and his shoes confiscated. Still, something about his shoes was a possible fit with the forensics at the scene.

A particularly deeply rooted weed was resisting her efforts to get pull it up. She yanked several times at it using both hands and almost tipped herself over when it finally came free. She had little affection for this type of deep-rooted resistance – in weeds or in personalities.

So who wears trainers? Answer: everybody under about 50 and more than half the population older than that. Sigh. But many people who owned them didn't wear trainers in the middle of a normal weekday. Office workers, retail sales assistants, nurses – most working people – wore shoes suitable for the job. No school children wore their trainers at that time of day either. Except for gym classes, of course. She tended to wear her own trainers at weekends. She had been wearing them before changing into her wellies for gardening, and she'd be wearing them again when back inside.

She glanced at her watch. She gathered the pile of weeds into her trug and hauled it to her garden waste bin for collection. No more avoiding what she had to do. She headed inside.

'Hi Bettina', she typed. Looked at it, decided it was too informal, suggesting she was using the fact they knew each other. She deleted it.

'Dear Bettina.' Not much better. Deleted it, too.

Maddie sat back in her office chair. A comfy one with arm rests and a tall back, chosen with care. It had been her Christmas present to herself as a reaction when Wayne had given her a new big flat-screen television. Since he was the person who watched television in their family and had been agitating for a television like this, she felt she deserved a new office chair. In retrospect, there was a hint of retaliation in buying it.

She stared out over her back garden, the areas where she'd freshly weeded that morning standing out beautifully. Encouraging. Each day she wasn't working, she vowed she'd do some work in the garden.

She wrenched her attention back to her laptop.

A CV. Yes, a lot of the information she wanted in this inquiry could be in the form of a Curriculum Vitae. She searched for the CV she'd submitted when applying for the job Romania eventually won. Not a comfortable memory. Her boss had 'known' Maddie would be given the job so had suggested Maddie need only construct a basic CV. Maddie cobbled it together one evening for submission the next day. In retrospect, it was an extremely foolish decision. But now was different. She figured it was best to start from scratch without the pall of what had happened that time tainting the present situation.

She typed, 'CURRICULUM VITAE, Madeleine Joy Brooks'. Dated it. Next line, 'A Report compiled for Bettina Rossmore on the occasion of a Human Relations Inquiry.'

She sat back. Yes. Totally formal.

Date and place of birth.

Early education.

University awards. That was fun to remember.

Bachelor's degree and Master's degree. First class honours. How amazing that had been at the time. Even now, it looked damned good in black and white all these years later. What did it mean? Just that she'd worked hard. Worked very hard for it.

She and Wayne were a couple by then, living in a grotty flat with two flatmates. Planning on marriage once she'd finished her degree. Subsisting on vegetables from her parents' garden and noodles, with two meat meals a week. Wayne had been second guitar in a band that had a regular Thursday through Saturday gig as a warm-up act before a bigger name. They'd told themselves it was only until they were discovered. And it brought a small but regular income – on refection, the only time Wayne ever brought in a regular income.

Neither she nor Wayne had complained. They were young, healthy and they had their love to keep them warm. She smiled at the memory.

Next section: extra courses. Maddie had to find the proper names of all the short courses she'd taken hidden somewhere on her hard drive. Not all that important, but warranting a mention, so a list would do. Short courses either run by the department itself or elsewhere. After a productive half hour, she had it assembled. She looked at the list then made it into a table headed 'Courses: those attended and those presented'. That looked better. She'd produced a swag of courses over the years, mostly at conferences in the form of workshops. Another search and the list had expanded by half again.

She paused at how to handle her one and only job as a Probation Officer. Divide it up by time? Or by position? They were related concepts. She decided by position, starting when she was junior and ending with the responsibilities and authority she'd enjoyed before Romania. She began typing.

On the second re-write, she remembered her published papers. Relevant? Who knows, but they should be included; very few active Probation Officers had academic papers published internationally and she had three. The first was based on her masters' research; the second when she had to deal with a difficult case that required a search of the literature on the subject; after all that research, the writing up of the case was a natural. The third was administrative when she and her boss had co-authored a paper about their experience turning a full time position into two part-time positions as a job-share and thus enticing back to work a couple of bright young women Probation Officers who had quit to be home with families.

Later, after the fifth and final edit, she concluded the CV was better sent as an attachment to an email to Bettina than in the body of an email itself. As she read it through one last time, she remembered it should also go to the union, an easy addition. She'd send it as a BCC so that Bettina wasn't reminded about the union's presence, even though she could assume Maddie would be represented some time or other.

Now to the email. That could be a detailed chronological account using the notes she'd meticulously kept when she realised she had a real problem with Romania. The requests to re-write the court reports. The extra hours. The training she'd provided for four of the Service Officers and their reactions. The resultant reports, including how one officer's resultant report could be sent directly without editing. Romania's response.

It didn't take long. After pressing the 'send' button, she collapsed back in her office chair gazing down at her garden in the afternoon sunshine, exhausted. Weeding, she decided, was definitely easier.

Her phone rang. Shirley.

"Have you time for a coffee?" she asked. "I've just received a letter from Kathy."

That woke Maddie up. "Same place as last time? Half an hour?" And so it was arranged.

······●·●····

Maddie found Shirley seated in the window alcove they'd occupied the last time they'd met with several pages of a hand-written letter in front of her. Once Maddie had ordered her coffee, she sat opposite.

"Why a letter not an email?" she asked.

"She's a Luddite," Shirley said with a smile. "Thinks history will be the worse for people no longer writing letters. Besides, she's seventy-four years old."

Maddie was genuinely surprised. "She's worn well. I'd put her mid-sixties."

"She's wonderful, isn't she! She's only two years younger than me and looks ten years younger."

"Not at all," Maddie said gallantly. "The letter?" Safer ground.

"It's full of genealogical stuff you won't be interested in but I can give you what's relevant."

"I'm all ears," Maddie said after thanking the waiter who had brought her the cappuccino she'd ordered.

"First, she's having a grand time. As she always does. Kathy is so outgoing, she makes friends everywhere."

Maddie nodded. She saw her that way, too.

"She's met the distant cousins she's known about for ages. Was staying with them for a while and apparently treated like visiting royalty. But this is what I really wanted to tell you. The cousins and the cousins of cousins Kathy met are all Milhouse relations. Some had it spelled with an extra 'l' – Millhouse. But not a single one had the extra 'n', with or without the extra 'l'. Not only that, nobody has ever heard of Milhousens in the family tree." Shirley sat back.

Maddie leaned forward. This was very interesting indeed. "Did she contact the Milhousen family she knows about? Whatsisname's wife?"

"She said she tried but she'd been unsuccessful. The phone number he gave her didn't work. Or she wrote it down wrongly." Shirley smiled. "Probably the latter."

"That's it?"

"Heaven's no. Kathy's no slouch. She found some Milhousens in Cape Town in the White Pages and rang every single one of them. All four of them. They were all related to each other. German background. And none knew about any father with a daughter in the UK."

Maddie's thoughts were whirling. "This Milhousen you met, do you know his first name?"

"Sadly, no. I spotted him at the meeting. Mainly because he was a fresh face. But he wasn't introduced as a new member or a guest so that means he is a viable member. I know his name because Kathy told me it, but I don't think she mentioned his first name. Or I've forgotten it."

"You didn't recognise him from other meetings?"

"No. I'm positive I've never seen him before. A tall bloke, nice looking, I guess. Dressed very casually like I'd expect a South African to dress. Muscles bulging out of a short-sleeved shirt, you know the type. Like a farmer on the veldt."

"I'd like to know more about him," Maddie said, half to herself. "This whole story is odd. A stranger gives Kathy a very expensive plane ticket, nothing required in exchange. But to take advantage, she has to leave immediately. And pay for her return trip, I presume?"

"Yes, of course. The freebie was London to Cape Town."

They sat silently, both absorbed by the improbable story.

"What motivation…," Shirley started to ask.

Maddie spoke at the same time. "Is there any record of your meeting? Minutes?"

"Yes, of course."

"Including names of attendees?"

"Some. New member, guests so they could be introduced. And anybody who spoke at the meeting."

"No Milhousen?"

"I'm not totally sure. I know there was a small discussion when Kathy used her cousins in South Africa as an example of glitches that happen when assembling a family tree." She looked at Maddie. "I can contact our secretary, if you want."

On her way home, Maddie assessed why she was following up on this. She decided it was partially because she had the time at the moment, but mainly because of the incongruity of Kathy – of anybody – being given such a freebie, coupled with having to cough up for the return ticket. That combination was in itself interesting. Kathy was probably thrilled to be making a trip she must have wanted to make for some time, plus, given she was a retired teacher with limited means and South Africa was so far away, she would most likely believe this was her one and only opportunity for a visit there. It had to be made as worthwhile as possible. That might mean a long trip to take full advantage.

Maddie needed Kathy's testimony for Henry's sake. But it looked as if Kathy would not be returning back to the UK with any alacrity.

Chapter Fourteen

Maddie rummaged through her wardrobe looking for an outfit to wear to the barbecue at the Dymocks'. She checked the forecast for the umpteenth time: it still said sunny during the afternoon and 22 degrees, down to 21 by 6pm with a few scattered clouds. It looked like she could wear summer clothes but with something to put over her shoulders if the temperature went any lower than forecast. She swished her work clothes to one side of the clothing rail to assess what was suitable. She had few casual clothes other than jeans and t-shirts. All right for someone in Jade's age group to wear to the barbecue. Not her.

Her final pick of a knit top in pastel blues and greens determined wearing pale blue trousers over white sandals and carrying a white cardigan and her summer white shoulder bag. Yes.

Wayne was always a problem. He despised fussing over clothes at the best of times, finally agreeing to wear beige cargo pants and a collared polo shirt in a dark blue. Even Jade seemed relieved he was wearing more conventional clothing than usual.

Jade had put on black jeans as Maddie predicted, and over them she was wearing a sleeveless black t-shirt, but a new one with a swirl of gold sequins in front. Youthful, pretty and almost summery. The first non-plain black non-long sleeved top Maddie had seen on her daughter in too long. She had on eye makeup but no lipstick and her natural freckles were showing. Fingers crossed the Goth period was fading.

The Brooks family arrived at Ham Common just after four-thirty. The afternoon sunshine on the Dymock house highlighted the last remaining but still magnificent blooms of a gigantic wisteria which almost obliterated the white render of the substantial two storied house. They approached the formal portico and saw the door was open.

"Come in, come in," Sharon called from somewhere within. "Go straight through to the back garden." She appeared briefly to give air kisses to Maddie and Jade and a perfunctory hug for Wayne waving them towards a wide terrace outside at the back.

Already about twenty people were talking in small groups, wine glasses in hand. Donald came over to welcome them, shepherding them into a conservatory to one side of the back of the house where wine, glasses and various nibbles were laid out.

Jade disappeared with Freya; Wayne joined a group of men talking football and Donald turned his attention to Maddie.

"I really like this house," she said to him. "It's absolutely delightful from the street, lovely and airy inside and these extensions here in the back are modern, beautiful and useful." She paused. "Sorry, I'm gushing. But I do love it."

"A family house. Grandparents, then parents and finally me. I'm lucky."

"You are indeed," Maddie agreed with enthusiasm. "But look what you've done back here. These extensions are recent, I presume. And a gorgeous blend in keeping with the rest of the house. Besides being up to the minute in style."

"I think you're wasted as a Probation Officer," Donald said. "You should be in real estate."

She held up her glass to clink with his. "I'll drink to that."

"You have a lovely daughter," he said. "Intelligent, slim, athletic and stunning looking. She must make the boys spin in their adolescent angst."

Maddie was startled. He was talking about Jade? Her Jade? Skinny, almost no hips or boobs, straight badly died black hair, shy. Looking almost pre-pubescent. What planet was he on? "Well, thank you, Donald," she said. "I guess a mother sees her teenaged daughter as just a slightly older little girl."

He gave a hearty laugh. "Yes, there's the little girl still in her – long may it last."

"It's lovely our two daughters are such good pals."

He raised his glass to her. Maddie clinked glasses, just ever-so-slightly disturbed.

"Your work must be interesting," he said. "And I hear you're involved with that guy who attacked one of our schoolgirls way back when. Freed rather briefly, I gather, and now back inside after our little murder. Very sad. I'm not sure about releasing sex criminals into the community."

Maddie cursed Jade for talking about what should be totally private. Cursed herself for trusting her. Then realised Freya was often at home with Jade. Freya. Dammit. A direct conduit straight to her. She kicked herself. She'd have to be much more discreet.

She decided not to get into a debate about the probities of parole. "My work is interesting, and I do meet some famous, or rather, infamous people," she said. "Yes, the awful murder of the young schoolgirl. The police have some suspects. Given the schoolgirl attacker of yore is back in prison, I guess we can assume he's on the list." She smiled, knowing she hadn't given him a single morsel of new information.

"I gather you've had some trouble at work," he said. "Hope it's not serious."

Proof Freya had been talking. "Nothing a good temper tantrum won't cure," she said lightly then decided to divert the conversation before it got awkward. "I hear you descend from one of William the Conqueror's knights."

"Not proven, but probable," he said. "Those times are fascinating. Our name, Dymock was spelled various ways back then like Dymoke or Dimmock. It's a combination of two words: 'Dim' means fort or manor and 'ock' comes from the old English word for oak. So, Dymock is Oak Manor."

"Old English, not French."

"Interesting you should say that. History records a Dimmock Manor in Lincolnshire was owned by a Nicholas de Dimmock about a hundred years after William the Bastard invaded. It's quite possible that Nicholas's great great grandfather was a knight who was awarded Dimmock Manor by a grateful William. Thus Nicholas was known as de – 'of' or 'from' – Oak Manor."

Maddie laughed politely along with Donald. "I guess genealogy has passed me by," she said. "Not that I'm incurious about where I've come from, but because when you're descended from peasants, nobody records much of anything."

"Oh, I'm sure there are many famous Brooks' ancestors," he said.

Sharon called him to start the barbecue and he was away before Maddie could reply that Brooks would have been the name of Wayne's ancestors, not hers.

She stood in the conservatory doorway looking out over the scene. She spotted Jade and Freya in a group of young people sitting on a grassy spot under a large apple tree near the Dymock's small curved swimming pool; Wayne was now talking to an attractive young blonde woman on the terrace with groups forming and re-forming around them and Sharon and Donald were fussing with food near the barbecue.

They were an attractive couple. Sharon was tall and slim, still looking like the model she once was and Donald was muscular, with his forearms bulging under the short sleeved shirt he was wearing over long khaki shorts and trainers. He looked like an Aussie, even though it was Sharon who was born in Australia. Actually, he looked every inch of how a gym teacher should look.

The golden couple turned to make their way towards Maddie, joining her at the top of the steps into the conservatory. "Going to give a little speech," he said with an apologetic smile.

Maddie got the message. "I'll just join the throng." She spotted Wayne again and made her way to him, telling him Donald and Sharon were about to speak to them all.

"Friends," Donald said in a voice she could imagine he could use to quieten a gym full of unruly teenaged girls. "We've invited you here today so we can tell you about some plans of ours. Plans about what we're about to do in the near future." He turned to Sharon and, with one arm, hugged her to him. "My dear wife, as you know, is in the fashion business. She's just been offered a wonderful opportunity to transfer across the pond. She's to be the collection manager for her firm in New York City."

People reacted with clapping, moans and 'oh, no's.

"Of course, we didn't tell anybody, including the upper management until we knew I could get a position in New York as well. I'm no house-husband."

Laughter.

"And, I'm here to tell you, come September, I'll be starting as a phys ed teacher with a private Episcopalian school on Long Island. Sharon will start her Manhattan job and Freya hasn't made up her mind yet. She's applied to various universities here and we're encouraging her to apply over there just in case she wants to join us."

Maddie searched for Jade in order to see her face but too many people were in the way. How had Freya kept this secret? She'd know Jade would be devastated.

Donald was talking again. "Yes, it will mean leaving ole Blighty, but we're not selling up here. Who knows how we'll like it over there? And who could give up this?" He held out his arms to encompass his manor, oaks or no oaks.

Of course, from then on, the only topic of conversation was this surprising announcement.

Maddie took her too-full plate of food over to one of several picnic tables on the grass near the pool. She wasn't a plate-on-your-lap sort of eater at the best of times. Especially not when she was wearing this particular knit top. She joined several others who felt the same way. When she walked over to replenish her wine glass, she again paused at the doorway of the conservatory. Now, the sun was more westerly and soaking the world in yellowing light. Donald was again at the barbecue cooking yet more steaks, his light brown hair now a burnished gold.

She stared. No. No, it couldn't be. She broke out in a cold sweat. Looked away. Looked back. Tried to banish the thought. Donald. Late sunshine highlighting his hair. Interested in genealogy. Looking now, in his shorts and trainers and at the barbie, like an Aussie. Or, looking like a farmer on the veldt.

Maddie grabbed another glass of red and headed back to the table. The conversation was back to New York City, ex-mayor Rudy Giuliani, crime and American politics. She joined in, all the while watching out for Wayne. When she spotted him, he was leaning over Sharon who was arching back as far as she could. Maddie leapt up and headed over to rescue her.

"Hi, Wayne," she said slightly loudly. "Sorry, Sharon, I'm here to take the boy home."

Grateful eyes met hers. "See you soon, Wayne. Lovely to have had you here."

"Evening's only sh – started. Haven't had food yet," he said, tipping his glass up and finishing whatever it was.

Maddie took the glass. She could smell it. Whisky. Probably neat.

"We're off home," she said firmly. Into his ear, she said, "You're drunk. Okay? Time to head home." She spotted Jade and signalled her to help. The two of them marched Wayne to the car and threw him into the back seat. Maddie mentally counted the glasses of wine she'd imbibed and decided to pay strict attention to her driving and to keep off the main roads.

"Dad, you're disgusting," Jade said, struggling to shove his legs in so she could close the door. "Ruining what was a really good party. Why did you have to drink so much?" Her voice rose in anguish. "Tell me that! Why, bloody, why?"

Wayne answered with a crescendo-ing snore.

Jade turned to her mother. "Why can't he be more like Donald?"

Chapter Fifteen

The next morning Maddie found it thoroughly therapeutic yanking out the biggest, deepest rooted weeds. Somehow being angry at Wayne helped in some stupid way. Her anger now suitably quashed, she looked back at her efforts with some satisfaction and decided to call it a day.

In the cold light of morning, her tying Donald Dymock to the stranger who financed Kathy's trip seemed an over-reaction. He had muscles (totally appropriate for a gym teacher); he was fascinated by his own genealogy (like thousands of others) and, besides, he was wearing trainers not farmer's boots. Duh. She really needed to get a grip. Focus.

She had two things in her life that were top priority: preparing psychologically for the Wednesday meeting with Bettina and the union rep and, for Henry's sake, gathering the facts around little Linsey Benton's murder. She'd keep on with her attempts at making contact with Kathy, for sure, but she needed to do something active about Brody Frederickson.

Jade had complained over and over again to her mother that they'd never be invited back to the Dymocks. And now her time with the Dymock family was limited, she was doubly furious at her father's behaviour. Maddie was well aware it was displaced annoyance that Freya hadn't warned her ahead of time about her family's plans.

"Is Freya planning on applying to American universities?" Maddie had asked Jade earlier.

"She says not," Jade said. "But I always knew we wouldn't end up at the same college. She's applying to places like St Andrew's in Scotland and Imperial College London. Oxford and Cambridge, of course. She'll never get selected for any of those."

"Why? Is she not being realistic?"

"She's just giving her parents bragging rights. You know, 'my daughter is weighing up whether Oxford or St Andrews would suit her'." She'd bent over and stuck her finger half way into her mouth, saying, "Yetch."

Maddie had laughed.

Once out of her wellies, she looked at the time and rang Shirley. They arranged to meet at ten the next morning. Usual place.

Wayne appeared looking like he always looked after tying one on.

"Breakfast?" Maddie asked brightly. And deliberately.

He looked even more nauseous, if that were possible. "Black coffee," he said. "No. Forget it. I've got to get going."

"You've had three calls from someone called Chrystal Morley asking where you were." She handed him the note where she'd written the name and number.

He nodded. "Singer. Promised her work today." He straightened, grabbed a jacket and ran to his car.

Maddie smiled wryly. Nothing like a new singer, presumably young and pretty, to motivate a hung-over middle-aged man.

She pulled up the Horscliffe website on her phone. She clicked on 'teachers' and found each had provided a short bio with a photograph. Good.

· · • • • • • • · ·

"Hi Shirley," Maddie said when Shirley sat down opposite her. "Can I show you a photograph of someone?" She handed her phone to Shirley with Donald Dymock's photo enlarged so it filled the screen. The bios on the school site had obviously demanded formal studio shots. Donald was staring into the camera with a serious expression, dressed in suit and tie, and the black and white photo did nothing to express his personality. Just like all the other photos of teachers.

"Who is it?" Shirley asked.

"Anything recognisable about this chap at all?"

Shirley fumbled for her glasses hanging on a strap around her neck. She peered closely at the screen.

"I presume this is either your client or Kath's benefactor."

"You've seen both," Maddie said, only now realising Shirley was absolutely right. There were two middle aged men they had in common.

Shirley slowly shook her head. "Can't say I've ever seen this particular chappie ever before." She handed the phone back to Maddie. "Sorry. I guess you had a theory I've just shattered."

Maddie laughed. "I found this picture on the net and thought I'd see your reaction. I don't think it's particularly illustrative of the man I know. Too formal. A mug shot with suit and tie."

"So you had hopes this was Milhousen?" Shirley asked. "I was down in the middle of the church hall when the meeting broke up. I didn't see his face clearly at all. My only impression of him was that he was tall – certainly taller than most yet without looming over people – and he had the muscles of a ... oh, I don't know, some sort of athlete. Not a weight lifter or anything like that. Rugby maybe? Tennis?"

Maddie pointed to her phone. "This fellow has muscles. That's really why I wanted to show him to you. But that's just about the only clue." She put the phone back into her bag. "Now, Shirley, you have some news about Kathy?"

"She's on her way to Pretoria now," Shirley said, "to stay with yet more rellies. What a wonderful trip this is turning out to be. I'm so happy for her."

Maddie agreed while inwardly cursing. "If you ever can contact her, would you let her know I'd really appreciate it if she could give the police a ring? Or drop them a note?" She handed Ethan's details to Shirley and explained how Henry was back in prison. "I can't see how he could have committed the murder given it happened when he was in your charity shop."

Shirley looked uncomfortable.

"What's wrong, Shirley?"

"I didn't know he was that awful sex offender," she said, looking down. "I'm sure Kathy didn't know either."

"He has paid his debt to society," Maddie said stiffly. "You don't want him to be punished for a crime he could not have committed, do you?" She forced herself to calm down.

"How can you work with such a person?" There was anguish in Shirley's voice.

"Because he is a person. And I can do my bit to see his life is as worthwhile as possible. But all that is about the crime he was convicted of some years ago, not a crime he could not have committed recently."

"Yes, I see," Shirley said in a small voice. "And I do take your point." She sighed. She got up from the table, in spite of not having finished her coffee. "And I do trust you, Maddie. I just find it very confusing."

Maddie sat, somewhat non-plussed at Shirley's reaction to Henry. But Shirley was voicing an opinion about child sex abusers held by, most likely, a majority of people in the UK. In the world.

As Maddie finished her coffee, she reflected on her own journey, the part concerning Henry, at least. A decent man. A middle-class man who shared many of her own hopes and aspirations, and, yes, prejudices. An educated man. In other circumstances, a man she would feel happy to invite to dinner. And her discomfort about his guilt. She accepted he was convicted; but, given the evidence, had she been a juror back then, she was not sure if she would have convicted him. She was only too aware of the minds of twelve-year-old girls. And how difficult it would have been for any non-psychopath to carry off a normal social evening after having committed such an atrocity, putting his job at risk if not his liberty, to say nothing about what it did to the child.

Her phone rang.

The union rep. He introduced himself as David Player. "Thanks for copying the email to me, Madeleine. Any chance you could pop in before Wednesday?"

Her car was parked behind John Lewis; his offices were walking distance away "I'm in Kingston right now, David. Should I come over straight away?"

As Maddie set out to walk to the union's offices, she felt almost weak at the knees. Shocked deeper than she'd realised about Shirley's reaction to Henry's background. Such a primitive reaction. She tried to shake it off but couldn't. As had gone through her mind when seeing Shirley's reaction, if she'd been on the jury, she would have had severe doubts about the child's story. Not because of facts, but how she told the story. And that had been years before she was assigned to his case.

If she delved down into the details of the case now, would her reaction be the same?

Another thought pierced her equilibrium. The police had automatically thought Henry was implicated in Linsey's murder because of the similarities of the two crimes and the proximity of where he lived and, of course, the fact that both girls went to Horscliffe. A natural reaction. But using that same argument took her to a new perspective. What if Henry had been wrongly convicted of orally raping Geneva Hopworth? If both crimes were committed by the same perp, he must be guilty of the second, much worse, but similar, crime. But what if he was innocent of the first? Tying the two together clarified the answer. It meant Henry was in prison for a crime he did not commit.

She paused before she entered the building where the union had its offices. She had a moral duty to look into it. At the moment, and who knows for how much longer, she had some of that most precious of commodities, time.

A few minutes later she was sitting across from a young man with the deep voice she recognised from their phone conversation.

"I like that you've included your CV as reference. Mostly because it's remarkable. Extraordinary. I have one question about this CV of yours," he said, holding a printout of it in one hand. "With these qualifications, why didn't you ask for a review when Romania was given the job instead of you? Your CV is twice as impressive."

Maddie warmed to him. "I just accepted they wanted someone other than me. Simple."

"You could have asked for a review. I wish you'd discussed it with us."

She shrugged. "It didn't even cross my mind. Sorry."

"No, I'm the one who's sorry. I think, maybe, I should write an opinion piece in the next newsletter about the various times members should let us know something is happening. Keep it all theoretical, but use this instance as an example." He put the CV down. "Okay, let's talk about what precipitated this whole scenario we find ourselves in now. The tipping point incident. Tell me in your own words."

She found herself talking it all through. He took copious notes. Her resentments at being asked to do so much work out of hours; the distain with which she was treated by Romania. Reaching what he'd called a 'tipping point' after which she threatened to work to rule. And all the detail about the Service Officers and her attempts to educate them and the resultant explosion by Romania.

"I recorded a conversation I had with her."

He looked troubled. "She knew she was being recorded?"

"I was on my landline; impossible to record a conversation on it. But I had my mobile phone on so it recorded my side of the conversation, not hers, of course. But you can get the gist if you want to hear it."

His face cleared. "Yes." He paused. "What a very good idea to turn your phone on. Do you have it here?"

Maddie pulled her phone onto the desk between them and they both watched her end of the conversation. One-sided maybe, but, as she knew, it spoke volumes. She felt only slightly guilty about the explanatory extension to the conversation.

"Thanks for letting me hear it, Madeleine," he said. "Keep it safe, okay?" He touched his notes. "I can go over these later and ring you if I can't make sense of them. I want to be fully briefed when we go into that meeting on Wednesday. Know as much about it as you do."

Driving home, Maddie realised her mood had lifted knowing someone was batting on her side. Still not confident, and slightly surprised she found such a young man a comfort, she did feel as if she could walk into Bettina's office with her head held high. Somehow going over it all reinforced her judgement. Confirmed, to herself at least, that her actions had been appropriate.

She arrived home to laughter coming from the kitchen. Jade, Freya and a tall young man.

"Oh, hi, Mum," Jade said while her face and neck flushed red. "This is Brody Frederickson."

Chapter Sixteen

Maddie stared at the young man. "Nice to meet you, Brody," she made herself say, furious with her daughter. What had Jade been thinking inviting a murder suspect here?

Jade, her face flaming, turned to her mother. "I know what you're thinking, Mum. But things aren't as simple as you like to think."

Maddie gave a wry smile at that comment and weighed up whether to get into the whole sex with under-aged girls thing. And immediately dismissed it. Not appropriate. But there were other ways. "I think the police are more interested in the murder than anything else," she said looking at Brody, wanting him to realise she was telling him the sex thing was not important. At least at the moment. "Better to face up to everything if you're innocent."

"If?" he said, his voice a growl.

"Yes, 'if', young man," she said, squaring her shoulders. "Of course, 'if'."

"Shit on you," he said, shoving his face inches from Maddie's, his voice rising. "I don't have to take this. You can bloody well think what you want, but the cops are never straight. Not ever. If they want to take it further, they'll bloody have to find me." He whirled out of the room and slammed the front door. Freya and Jade followed, yelling his name.

Maddie collapsed onto one of the kitchen chairs. How did that deteriorate so quickly? Because he was guilty?

That's when she did the math. Seven years ago, Brody was ten years old. She dropped her head onto her hands. Could a boy of ten orally rape a girl who was a couple of years older than he was? More basically, would a child of ten have been sexually motivated?

Unlikely.

That is, given the similarities in the two crimes were overwhelming and thus had both been committed by the same perpetrator. Using this logic, Brody Frederickson was not the murderer.

Maddie found her mind drifting back to her reaction to the details of that original oral rape. She thought of twelve-year-old Geneva Hopworth and her ordeal at the school gym. The child had suffered, Maddie had no doubt about that. Medical testimony showed bruises where no bruising should be. No DNA evidence, but nobody doubted she had been orally raped.

The child's courtroom testimony at Henry's trial had been by video link and the court's questions had been put to her by a trusted female psychologist rather than the lawyers. To Maddie, at the time mother to ten-year old Jade and eighteen-year old Olivia, young Geneva had sounded unsure. That tone of voice was significant. If either of her daughters had used it with her, she'd know something wasn't as it seemed. Further, at the end of the questioning, the child became defiant. Not that Maddie would wish psychological stress on any child, especially one who had undergone such an ordeal at the hands of an adult male, but the defiance felt like a loud protest for her lie to be believed. Anyway, that's what her own kids would have done if a lie was being questioned.

But, what had bothered her ever since was, what lie? The child had been raped. That was not a lie. Its timing was not in dispute, sometime between most students and teachers leaving the school and her arrival home. No lie there. Henry had used the showers. No lie there. She was after her shoes. Certainly her shoes were found near the gym. By Henry. The rape took place at the gym ... or did it? The child said it was Henry ... but displaying those tell-tale signs as if a lie lay somewhere....

A doubt. Maybe even a reasonable one.

Maddie had to do something about it. Wondered why she hadn't protested at the time. Knew she'd gained in becoming confident in her own powers of deduction since then. It seemed pathetic to say she hadn't protested back then because of a lack of self-confidence, but she certainly did not feel that way any longer.

Geneva would now be nineteen or twenty. A young woman. Maddie knew her parents had withdrawn the girl from Horscliffe well before the trial. To get away from it all, her parents had sent Geneva as a boarder to a girl's school somewhere in Buckinghamshire, at least that was what Olivia had remembered.

Maddie entered 'Geneva Hopworth' into a google search, pleased the girl wasn't a Susan Smith or even an Olivia Something-or-other. Geneva's Facebook page came up first in the search and she clicked on it. A more mature, but easily recognisable Geneva was in countless photographs on her Facebook page. Maddie scanned the news feed. Geneva loved her new job. Great people to work with. Adored being part of the mayor's office. Enjoyed being in the heart of London which was 'made for young people' or so she claimed. Etc. Oh, how Maddie loved google and Facebook for making searching for someone so absolutely easy. Oh, how Maddie hated the idea that her daughters, especially immature Jade, could be found so easily.

She realised she hadn't checked Jade's Facebook account for ages. Although they messaged each other at times, she berated herself she'd been distracted from this most imperative of parental duties.

Jade's site was also full of pictures, mostly of Freya, Kim, the other girls she knew and herself. None of Maddie or Wayne, she was grateful to see. In her last little talk with Jade about social media, she had pointed out how dangerous it would be if some disgruntled crim was able to trace her. That little discussion must have been effective.

Jade's comments were universally about only two subjects: school and stars, that is, stars in the movies and popular music. Thank goodness.

Maddie looked up a number and entered it into her phone.

"The Mayor's Office, Samantha speaking. How can I help?" said a young voice.

"Geneva Hopworth, please," Maddie asked in her 'official' voice.

"Which department?"

"She's a receptionist, I think." A wild guess for a young woman without tertiary qualifications.

"Hold on," the voice said. "Putting you through now."

Maddie clicked off. She grinned. Too easy.

Jade came in. "Look, I know what you're going to say, all right? It was Freya who said he could come back for a coke. My house was closer than hers, okay? Like, it was just ordinary." She glared at her mother.

"Calm down," Maddie said. "Just tell me without yelling."

"Why did you have to tell your bloody friend in the police about Brody?" Jade's face was contorted in her anger.

"I didn't."

"Don't bloody lie to me, Mother!"

"Stop swearing!" Maddie could feel her own frustration building. She didn't need this right now.

"You're pathetic," Jade said, swinging away and running up the stairs. A minute later loud music filled the house. Jade's usual protest.

Chapter Seventeen

The next morning, once Jade and Wayne had left, Maddie rang the Mayor's Office again. This time, she allowed the call to be put through. The voice of another young woman said, "Geneva Hopworth here. How may I help?"

"Hi Geneva," Maddie said. "Mrs Brooks here, Jade's mother. I'm on my way up to London and Jade said you now work at that wonderful modern City Hall."

"Yes, I do." She paused. "Jade Brooks?"

"You two went to the same primary school although Jade was younger. But you both took ballet lessons together." She rushed on. Jade had only lasted a couple of weeks. "Any chance I could treat you to a coffee this morning? Is there a coffee shop there?"

"Ah, yes," the young woman said. "Okay. Ten is when I have my break. But I'll only have fifteen minutes."

"Great," Maddie gushed. "How do I get there?"

Geneva proceeded to tell her to go through security at City Hall then descend the spiral staircase. She'd be waiting at the bottom at precisely ten.

Maddie's grin faded when she realised what her next steps would involve. She'd developed interviewing skills over the years she'd been a Probation Officer and she figured she'd have to be very careful which techniques she could use when meeting up with young Geneva.

Maddie headed for her clothes closet. First, dress the part. She pulled one of her navy blue corporate suits out of the wardrobe and a crisp white blouse and put them on. Low heeled office shoes with a matching shoulder bag completed her costume. For costume it was, albeit playing a familiar role.

She hesitated once dressed and ready to leave. She was well aware she'd rushed into meeting up with Geneva as if the young woman could solve all Henry's problems. No, this visit with her would just be to initiate contact. No pushing. No direct questioning. Friendly and sympathetic. And to watch the kind of language Geneva used. Including body language. Was it a wild goose chase? Maybe. Even, probably. But still worth it.

She headed for the train station. Taking one of the more direct trains, she soon was in Waterloo Station with only a ten minute walk to City Hall. The building was an architectural wonder, looking something like a gigantic glass helmet, slightly canted to one side. A sight to behold and one that made her smile. She'd never been inside before and felt like a tourist as she approached the entrance.

Once in, she found herself gaping at the magnificent spiral staircase that wound its way up ten or more stories in the grand atrium of the building. But she stopped gawking; she was on a mission. Soon she was through security and heading down into what she expected to be a basement. Instead she found herself in a large curved room overlooking an outdoor amphitheatre. Long tables with gaily coloured chairs were placed end-on to the floor to ceiling windows. She was pleased to have arrived before Geneva so she could orient herself.

Two minutes to ten, Geneva walked down the curved ramp. She was now a blonde with a generous figure dressed in a bright floral frock and wearing high heels that must be making her nervous she'd fall at any moment, poor girl.

Maddie waved. "Hi, Geneva!"

"Hi, Mrs Brooks!" She matched Maddie's tone which told her this young woman was still in the process of maturing, most likely fighting a fragile sense of self-confidence. Her own self-confidence swelled. She could deal with this sort of young woman.

"You lucky thing, working here," Maddie burbled. "You must be the envy of every young woman for miles around."

Geneva blushed. "I guess that's why Jade told you I worked here, is that right?"

Given that Maddie was not sure Jade even remembered Geneva other than because of the notoriety of the trial, she had to change the subject quickly. "Coffee, my dear? I know you only have limited time but I so appreciate your spending it with me."

Once seated at the window end of one of the tables, Maddie sobered. "You do look every inch an up-and-coming, successful young lady," she said. "I hope you don't mind my saying so, but

I am so pleased that awful business when you were first in high school didn't scar you for life."

Geneva shook her head. "Never think back on it," she said a bit forcefully. "I hardly remember it, actually."

"Thank goodness for that. I guess you heard about another pre-teen who was murdered out our way not long ago."

Geneva shuddered. "Mum says, 'But for the grace of God'."

"Yes. Just a bit too similar." Maddie sipped her coffee, keeping her eyes away from Geneva's. This was the tricky bit.

"I'm so so glad Macgregor is back in prison," Geneva said.

"So you saw the similarity, too, did you?"

"Hard to escape it. Little kid about the same age as me; the same awful crime only worse; same suburb; even the same bloody school." She glanced at Maddie. "Sorry." Presumably for swearing.

"So you also think it had to be the same bloke."

"Of course it was the same bloke. The police must think the same. He was put back in prison. I'm glad he's there. He can rot in there for all I care." Her voice had risen. She became aware of it and whispered, "Sorry."

Maddie touched the young woman's forearm. "Nothing to be sorry about. And I do agree it has to be the same bloke. For all those reasons you just told me. However, there's one huge problem. Macgregor didn't do it."

Geneva stared at Maddie. "What do you mean?"

"There are witnesses who were with him for the exact time of the murder."

"No. Couldn't be."

"They saw him, talked to him for some time."

"Probably criminals like him."

Maddie shook her head. "Lovely people. Ordinary citizens like you and me. Not even connected with him in any way."

"Maybe the girl was killed a little later?"

"The girl's body was found quite soon so the doctor's estimate of the time of death was reasonably tight. And, besides, Macgregor was picked up by his daughter from a busy café just afterwards. He and his daughter – who was getting married the next day, by the way – had lunch in a posh restaurant where loads of people saw them. He was dressed up for his luncheon that morning."

Geneva was stunned. She stared out through the large windows of the café across to stone steps set in a long curve, the large amphitheatre immediately outside.

"But he was convicted."

Maddie was acutely aware Geneva was now talking about her own case. Interesting she hadn't said, 'But I know it was him.'

Maddie let the silence grow.

"He really couldn't have killed that girl?"

"No. He couldn't have done it."

"Why is Macgregor back in prison," she asked in a small voice.

"Because the principal witness is overseas. But she told other people about her conversation with Macgregor before she left. At the time, she was crystal clear. She talked about it to several of us. She'll contact the police when she's back. And they'll release him. For sure. It's impossible for a person to be in two places at once."

Geneva looked confused. She'd obviously realised the implications. If the same person who raped her, years later killed the girl, it could not have been Macgregor.

Maddie walked up the spiral ramp with Geneva and said her goodbyes, scribbling her email address on a scrap of paper. "Feel free to contact me at any time, Geneva. I've very much enjoyed our little chat. You do work in an amazing environment."

The young woman thanked her politely for the coffee although she still spoke in a small voice. Maddie felt more than a little guilty about further disturbing her.

Back on the ground floor, she turned to the massive spiral staircase just as Geneva would have expected her to do. She continued walking up the sloping ramp a full ten stories to the public viewing platform at the top. There, with half a mind, she noted the glorious view and dutifully took several pictures of London at her feet but her mind was stuck on the conversation she'd had in the café below.

Had Geneva harboured doubts of Macgregor's guilt all these years, even though she'd identified him? Guilt that had been apparently confirmed by the death of the schoolgirl in similar circumstances?

Had her doubts now been intensified?

Chapter Eighteen

Tuesday morning, Maddie was half way through checking their monthly credit card statement – not that she was all that good about remembering to do so on a regular basis, but the total this month was abnormally high – and found a large amount had been paid to their optometrist. Strange. She'd meant to get her eyes checked for her reading glasses but had not done so yet. Jade had perfect vision and Wayne had an antipathy about his deteriorating eyesight, preferring cheapie magnifying glasses from the Pound Shop rather than admitting he needed to have his vision properly assessed. A harmless middle-aged vanity, in Maddie's opinion.

"Are you finally getting new prescription glasses?" she called out to him. He was next door in their bedroom getting dressed.

"How did you know?" he asked, appearing at her home office door.

"Credit card," she said. "Can't sneak anything past me." She grinned at him.

"I, um, bought some contact lenses," he said. "So I can see when I'm working."

She was astounded. He'd been wearing his cheapie glasses last night and complaining he didn't have the right pair for watching television. "Are the contacts no good?" she asked.

"No. They're great. Makes a huge dif," he said, turning away.

"Why aren't you using them, then?" She was curious. Hundreds of pounds for contacts and he's not wearing them?

He looked embarrassed. "I bought them for work."

She narrowed her eyes. He was fibbing. "Where are they now?"

"At the studio."

"For heaven's sake, Wayne, if they make life better for work, they'll make life better for leisure, too."

"You're right," he said, brightening. "I'll bring them home."

"Wear them home," she said, turning back to the accounts.

It was only after she'd heard him leaving for the studio, she thought their conversation through. She shook her head. She must have caught him in the middle of some musical creativity and only half paying attention to her. Just wearing the new contacts in the studio indeed. Not able to admit he really did need proper glasses, contacts, whatever.

She wandered downstairs for a cup of something. Peppermint tea would do. No caffeine. Having all this spare time continued to feel odd. She mentally ticked off the various tasks she'd set herself before meeting with the HR person and the boss's boss, Bettina. Which was, gulp, tomorrow.

First, Shirley. Stuck there. Nothing to do at the moment. Or should she have a talk to Shirley about how she should not tell Kathy that Henry was a convicted child sex offender as it could influence her judgement. How would Shirley take it? As a criticism? Or could she see how it had influenced her own attitudes? Maddie shoved that one into the too-hard basket.

Second, Brody. Ethan now had that one firmly under control. Did she have any tag ends to untangle? Jade and her belief her mother had talked to Ethan – one of a series of too many things Jade believed that had little or no substance to them. Maddie would clear it up if ever an opportunity occurred. But she wasn't holding her breath.

Oh. It stopped her cold. She'd forgotten about the stepfather. Had Brody made up the story to divert the attention of the police away from him? But something niggled. A thirteen year old girl who was presumably having sex with an older boy. Not something that happened in middle-class suburbia, or, anyway, not that often because of parental oversight. Or something.

When a child has been sexually abused, she knew, sometimes the child becomes hyper sexual. Not that she knew very much about it. Was it a truism that a child who was sexually active at thirteen was hyper sexual? Not a topic she wanted to think about. But one she really should not ignore.

Her tasks. Yes. She was up to the third. What was her third? Something about the weekend Freya stayed … oh, yes. A romantic weekend away. Good for a marriage. She reached for the telephone.

After filling in her friend Caroline, a psychologist with the Probation Service in Ealing and a long-time friend, on all the shenanigans concerning Romania, Maddie asked about the cottage Caroline had inherited from her grandparents. What was it called?

"Briar Cottage," Caroline said. "I've just spent a weekend there. Mostly doing housework – it's ages since I'd been up there, but still it feels like I've had a weekend away. Thinking of accepting my offer?"

"Yes, actually. It was triggered by something I heard recently, about how any marriage needs a romantic weekend away every now and again. My acquaintance was talking about a short holiday in New York, of course, but it did put me in mind of your Woodley Bottom hideaway."

Caroline laughed. "Kind of stretching it, my friend, comparing my cottage in the depths of Oxfordshire to flying off to a glamorous location like New York. But tell me the dates and I'll see if I can fit you into its extremely busy schedule."

"I haven't even broached the topic with the Musical Genius," Maddie said, "but with no work, it will not be too difficult to fit whatever is available into my own extremely un-busy schedule. Around spending my time weeding the garden and waltzing off for coffee dates with friends, of course."

"Talking of coffee dates...."

After arranging to meet up on Thursday, the day after the dreaded meeting at work, both if she were still off work or back, Maddie, with some trepidation, rang Shirley.

"Shall we meet for coffee?" she asked in a soft voice.

"Usual place, three o'clock?" Shirley answered, equally quiet.

"See you there."

Maddie changed her shoes for her coffee date and put on some lipstick. She gazed at her hair. Needed a cut. And she had Bettina in the morning. Did she have time before meeting Shirley?

Maddie rang her hairdresser. No, she was busy right now, but, if only a cut, she could squeeze her in at, say, four-thirty. Maddie made the appointment.

She hung up the phone and looked at the time.

The stepfather. It niggled. She walked into her home office to consult Mr Google. She remembered the Gainlys last name, but what was his first name? She googled Linsey Benton and up came several news sources. While scanning them, she finally found an interview with the parents, Janine and Trevor. Trevor Gainly. She googled him and the same recent news items came up but below them she found a nugget. A Trevor Gainly – there couldn't be more than one, surely – was awarded car salesman of the year several months ago. The photograph confirmed it. So Trevor Gainly sold cars. In Kingston-upon-Thames. And she knew where that car yard was located.

When Maddie arrived at the coffee shop, Shirley was already seated with her coffee in front of her. Maddie waved and smiled before ordering her cappuccino at the service desk.

When she sat down, they both talked at once.

"Sorry…," Shirley said.

"My fault…," Maddie said.

The moment was perfect and they both visibly relaxed.

"You first," Maddie said.

"I was out of order last time," Shirley said. "It was the shock. I'd followed that case and been relieved when the man was sent to prison for some time. I'd obviously not recognised him when he came into the shop. Truly, when you said who he was, I almost fainted."

"I should have made it clear from the beginning," Maddie said, reaching over to lightly touch the back of Shirley's hand. "It's sort of a 'need-to-know' situation. We usually don't tell anyone what crime had been committed unless totally necessary, which is not often." She sighed. "I should have realised it was necessary this time. My fault entirely."

"Do you think he murdered the second child?"

"He couldn't have," Maddie said, looking Shirley in the eye. "The murder took place when he was in the shop, being served by Kathy."

"Strange," Shirley murmured, her eyebrows raised.

"You mean two nearly identical crimes in the same area not committed by one and the same person?"

Shirley's blue eyes widened. "He did do that awful thing to the first child, didn't he?"

Maddie gazed out the large window, watching cars manoeuvre through the streets, school children walking in twos or fours and more, cluttering up the footpath. She saw none of it. "He was convicted," she said, "largely because the child identified him."

"A truthful child?"

Maddie shrugged. "The jury believed her."

Shirley, the former teacher, looked at her sharply. "I see."

Maddie threw out her previously constructed introduction to the delicate problem of Kathy's reaction to Henry's crime. Instead she leaned forward and spoke directly to Shirley. "What shall we tell Kathy?" she asked.

"Or rather, when?" Shirley replied.

· · · · ● · ● · · · ·

Maddie bade Shirley goodbye outside of the coffee shop. She had three quarters of an hour before her hair appointment and she knew how she'd use it. She walked to the car yard.

She had peered into several cars, reading the list of attributes on the sheet of paper hanging in the window each time before a salesman walked over to her. Not Trevor Gainly.

"Lovely little beastie," he said with a grand toothy smile that split his face. "Goes like the wind."

"Nice coppery colour," Maddie said deliberately just to see whether the salesman's smile changed. It did, but it only froze momentarily.

"That it is," he said heartily. "Now what is it that you are looking for?"

Maddie thought fast. "Actually, these are used cars. I promised myself that when I did an upgrade I would buy new. Do you just sell used cars?"

The smile got even broader if that was at all possible, showing even more teeth. "My goodness, no. Let's go into the showroom and see the little beauties in there."

"I'm just looking, mind," Maddie said. "My husband is the one who does the buying of cars in our family." She smiled. Unfortunately, that silly statement was actually true. Her own car was the result of a more-or-less happy transaction when one of Wayne's mates had fallen on hard times and had to sell his car at short notice, and at a good discount. Maddie had no say in the matter, but given the car was significantly newer than the one she'd been driving, she'd accepted with good grace. No matter the colour.

Sure enough, Mr Trevor Gainly, master car salesman, was hovering over a small desk in the corner of a large glitzy showroom full of shiny cars. He wandered over to them. "Can I help?"

Toothy Grin paused. "I'm just showing this little lady our range. Hubby may be along later."

Gainly nodded wisely. In other words, not worth his while. "Let me know if I can add anything," he said, his disinterest plain.

With a quick glance at the time, Maddie asked if she could test drive a car of the same coppery colour as the one she'd admired outside.

Toothy looked sad. "I can drive you. Would that do?"

"Not me driving?"

"Well…" He shot a quick glance at Gainly who was busy shuffling papers at the small desk.

"Oh, I see," Maddie said. "It's new. What about that other one of the same colour? The used one. Could I drive that one?"

"Oh, yes. That one would be fine. But … did you want to?"

The poor man was thoroughly confused. Time to put him out of his misery. "Oh dear," she said, looking at her watch. "My hair appointment." She looked up at him with a sorry smile. "This will have to be postponed."

"Maybe come with your husband next time?" Toothy asked.

Maddie noticed Gainly's head come up. He'd been listening. He approached.

"My card," he said, shoving it into her hands. Maddie had a quick look at Toothy's face. Done by the master salesman.

As she sat with her hairdresser snipping away, Maddie reflected what she now knew. First, Gainly was a car salesman. Second, sometimes people are allowed to drive off; sometimes not. Therefore, sometimes a salesman could be away from the car yard. But Gainly was wearing a smart suit and very shiny shoes. Hardly the gear for murdering a stepdaughter at the muddy edge of the Thames.

· · · ● ● · ● · · ·

Wayne came in while Maddie and Jade were in the middle of dinner.

"What happened to you?" Maddie asked, shocked at Wayne's new haircut. "Did you fall into a threshing machine?" She grinned at him. "Don't tell me you did this deliberately." Some of his hair had been almost shaved and some remained that bit too long. It was a modern cut occasionally seen in rock bands, or, maybe, even younger wannabe fans.

Wayne blushed.

"It looks great, Dad!" Jade said. "Except for your wrinkles, you could pass for fifteen." She guffawed.

"Wayne, have you dyed it?" Maddie turned to Jade. "Would you believe, your father has dyed his hair."

"Sad," Jade said, shovelling the last of her spaghetti into her mouth.

Wayne spun on his heel and left, slamming the front door behind him.

Jade and Maddie looked at each other and burst into giggles that only grew in intensity.

When she could, Maddie gasped out, "It'll grow. That's all I can say to him when he returns." She wiped her eyes. "It had better grow!" Which set them off into a new fit of giggles.

Jade left to do her homework and Maddie sobered instantly. New contact lenses, dyeing his hair and a mod haircut?

When she stood, she reached for the chair back to steady herself.

Chapter Nineteen

Maddie awakened early. She turned off her alarm so it wouldn't wake Wayne and got up to shower feeling the luxury of having plenty of time. Her clothes, chosen the night before to convey sober professionalism, was the same outfit she'd worn to meet Geneva. It hung on a hanger off her wardrobe door. Navy suit, white blouse, new tights, matching low heeled shoes and small ruby pin she'd inherited from her grandmother. She headed to their ensuite to wash her newly cut hair and, afterwards, blow-dry it carefully. She glanced at her sleeping husband. His new haircut looked as ridiculous in the cold light of dawn as it had the night before. Totally inappropriate. But on his return home, she'd told him she'd merely been startled and apologised for being rude. She made him hot chocolate with a shot of whisky and he seemed mollified.

She eased herself into the hot shower, willing her muscles to relax. Letting the water beat against her back, her chest, each shoulder in turn. Concentrating on her breathing. Breathing in – in – innnn – breathing out – out – ouuuut – stop breathing. Repeat. And again.

By the time she was dressed, she figured her emotional equilibrium was probably as calm as it would be for the remainder of the day. The nice thing about the breathing exercise was its privacy – a private technique that could be done anywhere, silently and secretly. And, in a meeting, discreetly. And it worked. She padded downstairs in her stocking feet carrying her shoes.

Nothing with caffeine today. She made herself some peppermint tea instead. She knew she needed food, but anything she thought of, she instantly rejected. Finally, she made herself a yogurt smoothie with bits and pieces from the freezer. She drove to the meeting knowing she'd done everything possible to prepare for it, both with her documentation and her personal equilibrium.

David Player, full of smiles and bonhomie, was waiting for her in the foyer. He reminded her that he, as her union rep, was allowed to ask questions but never to answer any of Ms Rossmoor's questions, as everything would be, or should be, directed to Maddie. "But I can halt the proceedings if we need to talk about anything in private with you. You can, too. Okay?"

"I'm okay with it all, David." She felt a wave of panic and did two cycles of her breathing to settle herself down as they walked to the lift. They arrived precisely on time for the meeting with Romania's line manager whose secretary ushered them into her office.

Bettina Rossmoor rose from behind her desk and Maddie quickly introduced David before she could ask any questions about who he was or why he was there.

"You have sent me your CV, Madeleine," Bettina said, leaning across her desk and addressing Maddie but not David. "But surely you know that I already hold a copy. After all, you applied for the position now held by Romania Carlisle."

"It's different," Maddie started to say, then realised such a statement would only aggravate matters. "What I mean to say is that I unfortunately thought, back when I applied for the promotion, that you knew me, knew my work and...." She gulped, then slowed herself down. "And I had been told I'd been the only person recommended for the job. That was unfortunate as I had become complacent. If I had realised...."

"Yes, yes," Bettina said. "A cosy deal, it seems. Unfortunately, the premise was untrue."

"At the time, it seemed natural and I reacted accordingly," Maddie said. "But I am not complacent now, Bettina. I have sent you a full *curriculum vitae*, the sort I should have sent you back then."

Bettina picked up a folder. "Certainly heavier, for sure," she said with a wry smile. "You've included every little 2-day course, I presume?" One eyebrow raised.

Maddie took a deep breath. "Every 2-day course and everything more significant as well," Maddie said. "This time, I did it right. University qualifications, published papers, all the positions I've held in the job and every one of those 2-day courses I either took or taught." She smiled broadly and got a small smile in return.

"I did skim it," Bettina said, putting the folder off to one side. "Now, to the matter at hand." She folded her hands on the desk making it clear no paperwork would be involved. "You were bitterly disappointed you were not offered the job." It was said as a flat statement.

Maddie stared at her, waiting for a question.

Bettina frowned. "Speak to that."

Maddie flicked a glance at David who shook his head in the faintest of signals.

"I expected to be promoted, more fool me." Breathe in, in, innnn....

"So you deny you were disappointed?"

"Disappointed? Of course. Bitter? Not a jot. I was still doing my job," Maddie said, looking Bettina in the eye. "And I'm good at my job, as you know. I was continuing doing what I love."

Maddie stopped talking and let the silence grow.

Bettina sighed. She pulled the sheaf of folders and papers back in front of her. She pulled out something. Maddie recognised it. Her report. Finally. She shot a glance at David Player who gave her a subtle nod.

"Now you indicate there were some changes to your responsibilities. Changes to how you deal with Service Officers."

Maddie nodded. "As detailed in my report."

Bettina again put the report down, folded her hands on top of it and leaned across her desk. "I put it to you, Madeleine, that you resented these changes, that you actively fought against these new duties and that you resisted by threatening to 'work to rule'." She glared at Maddie.

"Before I answer that," Maddie said, "I'd like to ask a procedural question."

Bettina looked mildly surprised. "If it's on-subject, go ahead."

"Is it or is it not a duty of senior personnel to guide, teach and facilitate the learning of skills needed to do the job effectively and efficiently to junior personnel?" She winced at her own officiousness.

"The answer is obvious. Of course. Are you alleging you were rebuked for fulfilling this duty?"

"I am," Maddie said simply. Bettina had not read the report, or, to be generous, had skimmed it thus missing this vital point. She glanced at David. Out of sight from Bettina, he made a 'T' sign, the universal time out sign. "Bettina, I wrote about what happened in this regard. Should David and I run out for some coffees for us all while you have a look?"

She looked up, frowned briefly, then nodded. "Mocha for me," she said. "Best place is across the street at *Raney's*."

Once outside, David gave Maddie a little clap on her shoulder. "Way to go," he whispered even though nobody was around.

"I had my heart in my mouth," Maddie said while they waited for their order on the pavement sitting in thin sunshine outside *Raney's* – decaf for her and full throttle for David and Bettina. "I was implying she hadn't read the report. It could have gone either way."

"You read it correctly," David said. "She's probably been filled to overflowing with Romania Carlisle's righteous indignation, I bet, and her fury at your defiance of her express orders. It all fits neatly. You are deeply bitter at not getting her job, resulting in your taking it out on Romania with your insolent behaviour."

"So much so, she only skimmed my CV and the report?"

"To the point of embarrassment."

When they returned to Bettina's office, her desk was strewn with the print-outs Maddie had sent to her and the printer on the bureau behind her desk was busy with yet another.

"Thank you," Bettina said distractedly when she took the coffee. "Almost done."

Maddie sat quietly beside David, sipping her drink, her eyes defocused. She did a couple of cycles of her breathing technique although she felt calmer than she had felt since arriving into this office.

"I have a better picture now," Bettina said, again leaning forward on her desk. "I've just requested two reports from each of the Service Officers by email. One from two months ago and the latest one. I have already had a reply from one of the Service Officers." She held up a report.

"Agatha, yes. She's particularly receptive to instruction and probably always was a cut above the others in report writing," Maddie said.

"A significant difference between the two reports. The second one is satisfactory, the earlier is not."

"I agree," Maddie said. "And she responded well to the instruction. So much so, I've asked her to team up with one of the others who does not seem to understand what is needed even today."

Bettina nodded, still reading.

"Thank you for coming in, Madeleine, Mr ... um..."

"David is fine," he said.

"Yes, thank you. We have begun a process and you will hear from me as soon as possible."

"I am still off work?" Maddie asked.

"Oh, yes. We are merely at the beginning."

"Do you have any questions about the HR process?" David asked.

"The supervision, that sort of thing? I've done it before." Her voice was curt, more like the earlier part of the interview.

Maddie stood, taking that as the end. "Thank you for reading it all, Bettina," she said. And meant every word.

Chapter Twenty

Maddie was still keyed up when she arrived home. She did a few rounds of her breathing exercise before pouring herself a large glass of wine. Not that she needed it. Or so she convinced herself. Just in celebration. She sipped it then pushed it to the centre of the kitchen table. She'd finish it when Wayne came home. Celebrating with him was much more fun than when alone. She hadn't given a thought about dinner.

Jade arrived and headed upstairs as usual. Still no Wayne. Late the one time she really wanted him home. Maybe ring for a curry meal?

"Jade," she called up the stairwell. "If I order curry, what do you want?"

"Korma, as usual," came the faint reply. Yes. Jade's usual. Wayne's was Tandoori and hers Chicken Kali Mirch. No reason she couldn't order now.

As it happened, the curries arrived before Wayne did. She wrapped a towel around the bag of curries and rice to keep it all as hot as possible.

Where was the man? She took another sip of the wine. About half left.

Finally she heard the door open.

"Ready to eat?" she called out.

"Sorry I'm late," he mumbled. "Last minute practice."

She really did not want to hear about his day. Not when she had so much to tell him. She launched into it as she gave each meal a two-minute blast in the microwave. She called Jade, poured a glass of wine for Wayne and finally sat herself down. Her story of her day was up to when she and David Player left to collect coffees for the three of them.

But it was not lost on her that Jade seemed more interested than Wayne. "And that supervisor could see the improvement in the Service Officer's reports?"

"She certainly did. I was quite amazed she'd contacted them right in the middle of my interview."

Jade pushed her plate away. "Great meal, Mum. Shouldn't say that when you ordered it in, but they really do curries like they should be."

"Mine is a close second?"

Jade gave her mother a small smile. "It's history study tonight. I've invented a new way of studying. Record the important points from your notes then ask a question about it. Leave a space to think of a reply. Then record the reply. Then the next day and each day afterwards, I listen to the tape, fill in the blanks and then my own voice says whether it's right or not. Simple."

"Doesn't sound simple, but it does sound like a good idea," Maddie said, pleased their conversation was ordinary with no excess emotion. "Quite creative, really, Jade. Repetition is always the key to getting facts into the brain."

"That's what I thought," Jade said, dumping her plate and utensils into the sink. "So if you hear me talking to myself, don't call Mental Health."

Maddie saw Wayne's eyes on their daughter as she was explaining her new inventive way of studying. But he didn't smile when she made the quip about Mental Health. What was going on with him?

"Earth to Wayne," she said, snapping her fingers.

His eyes wandered to hers with a frown. "What's with you?"

"Get with it, Wayne, please. I'm in the middle of a crisis at work. Aren't you interested?"

He shook his head and bent over his curry. He spooned up another mouthful then pushed the half uneaten plate away. "Sorry. Didn't sleep so well last night." At that, he got up from the table and headed into the living room. The television went on. She followed him in.

"Wayne, remember how Donald and Sharon had their weekend in New York?"

He flicked his eyes at her. "Donald and Sharon?"

"The Dymocks. When we had Freya for the weekend."

"Oh. Yes, of course."

"Sharon thought it good for their relationship. I do too. I thought we could do the same. Not New York, of course, but take advantage of their thinking they owe us one. And with them leaving soon, we can take advantage. Jade could stay over with Freya."

"What are you talking about?"

"Caroline, at work? You remember her. We went to her wedding. One of them."

He nodded. They'd been invited to Caroline's second wedding. Wayne had met her then. She'd eloped, if people in their fifties can elope, for her third wedding.

"Caroline has a cottage in the country. Away from everything. Maybe we could take a few days...."

"Hey, hold on," Wayne said. "I can't take time off at a weekend. That's the only time I can depend on everybody turning up. You know that."

"Not a weekend necessarily," Maddie said. "I'm off work. We can take a couple of days anytime. Just imagine. A little cottage in a small village surrounded by countryside. Ambling through fields and woods. A cosy fire in the grate. Nothing to do but walk and read and talk about anything. It sounds like luxury to me. And it would be just you and me."

He touched his ludicrous haircut.

That did it. Things crashed around her. That damned haircut. The contacts. Being late when Wayne was always on time for dinner. A dinner cooked for him, served to him and the kitchen cleaned up afterwards while he luxuriated in front of the telly.

She rang Caroline. "I'm going to cancel our coffee date. Need to. Wayne doesn't want a holiday away." She wasn't sure she was making sense.

"Let's have a girl's weekend instead," Caroline suggested. "Drive up on Friday. Just the two of us."

"Sounds like heaven," Maddie said. And so it was arranged.

Maddie turned back to the kitchen. She took a deep breath. Let it out. Again. She looked around the kitchen with dirty dishes everywhere, her last bit of wine still in the glass. Wayne's abandoned dinner.

Tears pushed at her lids.

Chapter Twenty-One

Maddie woke disoriented. Her eyes were greeted with old fashioned roses on wallpaper that extended over the ceiling and instantly she knew she was in Briar Cottage, Caroline's Oxfordshire eighteenth century place-in-the-country. She stretched and listened.

Birdsong. Silence. More birdsong.

For the first time in what seemed a very long time, Maddie smiled.

She threw off the bedclothes and opened the casement window, filling her lungs with fresh country air that wafted in. It was cool, but leaning on the windowsill, cool felt good.

Beyond the garden, early morning sunlight filtered through the leaves of a stand of tall beeches – is that why the two villages were named Woodley? She could see the birds now, flitting to and fro, the only discernible movement.

She shut the window and put on her bathrobe. Smells of coffee were wafting up the stairwell. Coffee first, then a shower.

"Sit," Caroline said when Maddie reached the kitchen. "No talking allowed. Just coffee."

Maddie grinned and did as she was told. What a difference from her own chaotic breakfast times at home when she had to push two grumpy people out the door with some sort of food either in them or with them.

Caroline, on the other hand, was swimming in a sea of calm. Her greying hair flowed down her back in untidy waves, so different from the professional bun she habitually wore when she was seeing patients. Her bathrobe had seen better days, secured with an old tie belonging to … Maddie had to think. Bright blue with purple spots – that must be husband number two, the one who owned the nightclub. Good riddance to that one.

After breakfast, still in their dressing gowns, Caroline led Maddie to the back conservatory; silence abandoned, they clutched second cups of coffee.

"Okay, what's up?" Caroline asked as they sat in wicker chairs. "More trouble with that cow of a boss of yours?"

Maddie shook her head miserably. "Wayne trouble."

"What's he done now?" Caroline, who had finally found happiness in her third marriage, had little sympathy with wives who put up with nonsense.

Maddie closed her eyes. "Put it this way: suddenly taken to dyeing his hair with no discussion beforehand. Brand new, highly inappropriate and trendy haircut. Contact lenses that he kept 'for work'. I didn't know about them until I saw the credit card bill."

Caroline guffawed. "That just shows what happens when a man thinks with his littlest head!"

Maddie's eyes snapped open. "So it's not just me being paranoid?"

"Paranoid? If a patient of mine could not see in which direction those facts are pointing, I'd be recommending a brain transplant."

Maddie shook her head in response. This was no laughing matter.

"What's changed in your life?" Caroline, the psychologist, asked.

Maddie sighed. "Nothing. In anything that matters, nothing."

"Come on, Maddie, my friend. I know – the world knows – you're having trouble at work."

"I've always kept a healthy distance between work and home." She knew it sounded as if she were on the defensive, but it was the truth.

"Listen to yourself," Caroline commented, settling back in her chair.

Maddie slowed herself down. Of course the Romania situation would affect things at home. She sighed. "Okay. The extra assignments given to me by Romania had to be done after hours. One of my complaints. That meant, go to work, home, dinner, work at home, bed. Rinse and repeat ... nothing for Wayne other than a quick cuddle before sleep." She'd not been there for him. Not for ages.

"How long?"

"Almost since Romania became my boss. Quite a few months now."

"But it's different now. You're suspended."

Maddie thought long and hard about it. "Physically, I'm around a lot more, yes. But, I'm consumed with the situation, always going on and on about it. I must be the biggest bore ever."

"It's a huge thing, Maddie. Is Wayne being supportive?"

That stopped Maddie in her tracks.

Support. That was her role. Assigned by Wayne and his sensitive, creative musical and needy soul. She'd love to be supported by Wayne for once. Right now, she needed support.

"It's not just the emotional support problem. I … I am facing … I have to decide whether to throw in the towel or not."

"Give up work? You?"

"What can I do? If the authorities decide in favour of Romania, there'll be no choice."

"What does Wayne think about that?"

"When I mentioned it, he threw a hissy-fit."

"He's threatened," Caroline said decisively. "Maybe he'll be forced out of his comfort zone, finally have to earn some money. Actually get off his backside and take some responsibility for his family."

Maddie stared at her friend. "Is that the way you've seen him all these years?"

Caroline let silence be her answer.

Maddie put her mug down on the wicker table between them. She let the silence linger. She needed to think. "Can we continue this discussion after I've been out for a walk?"

Caroline leaned forward and touched Maddie's forearm. "I'll be here."

· · · · ●· ● · · ·

Maddie let herself out of the front door and walked down the pea-gravel drive. Across the lane, she spotted a path leading into the woods. Just what she wanted. A perfect place to analyse her life. Quiet, no people and she had the time for herself, an untold luxury. After all, that's why she came this weekend. She didn't allow herself to think about the romantic weekend she'd had to abandon.

Okay. Her marriage. She fell in love with Wayne shortly after she'd met him. He and his group had played at an outdoor venue on campus when she was completing her social work master's degree one sunny hot day. Maddie and about thirty other students were sitting in the shade of a large tree for the concert. Weird music. Sort of appealing, although Maddie wasn't a music aficionado. It was pleasant sitting outside doing nothing instead of figuring out the knotty problem of what she was to write up next for her thesis.

Afterwards, she continued to sit there, watching the musicians pack up. She hadn't realised she was the only one left until the dark haired boy who had played the lead guitar called out to her.

"Did we send you into a dwam?" He smiled a wonderful smile as he said it. A smile that lit up his face, changing him from average looking to appealing.

"Must have," she said, walking towards the group.

"We're off to the pub. Join us?"

And that was the beginning. Now, several decades on, with two grown up daughters and a fair few unsuccessful albums, he continued to make weird music that she still didn't understand. She was (perhaps, maybe) still working as a Probation Officer, a job she landed immediately she finished her university studies. And now he had bought himself contact lenses. Secretly. And his hair....

Yes, obvious what was going on. Big question: had it progressed or was he merely trying to impress somebody?

Her gut clenched.

The trees were old and stretched high above her forming a canopy of green. Undergrowth was minimal – far too little light, she presumed. This deep into the woods, even the birds were quiet.

The needy bit. She had to think about it. At first, she had a good salary coming in and he did not. She financed renting some studio space for him. She financed their house, or rather, she and the bank. She paid the credit card bills. She sent their older daughter to university and would contribute to their younger one's studies next year. Whatever Wayne earned went back into 'the business'. Or so he always said. And she had no doubts it was correct. Wayne periodically released CDs and DVDs of his music but never boasted about any great successes. Any. She assumed each was a flop but it was a subject that was not to be discussed. She knew he always felt there was always the next one coming, more innovative, more creative....

She'd been the strong one. She'd been the breadwinner. She'd been the giver. She did all the cooking. And the housework. And the gardening. And was the one to go to school concerts, meetings with teachers, games involving the girls and whatever else periodically had cropped up over the years.

An unfamiliar feeling welled up within her. It took a moment to identify what she was experiencing. Both her body and her mind were singing the same sad song. She listened. It was telling her something. Something important.

To run. Yes, for the first time in her life, she would like to run away.

Chapter Twenty-Two

Maddie talked a lot, those two days she spent with Caroline in rural Oxfordshire. She knew this was her only opportunity to do so without rancour. If she could only get her distress under control, she could maybe return home to take up her life without Wayne or Jade realising something momentous was happening. Maybe. Buy some time to get herself sorted. Even thinking about it caused her guts to protest, her heart to race and her skin to break out in periodic sweats, particularly at night.

Sunday, Caroline set to prepare a French *ragout* to cook in the slow cooker she kept at the cottage. They would be driving home straight afterwards.

"I love preparing this dish," Caroline said as she chopped fresh vegetables. "It's therapeutic. Then all afternoon the smells intensify, driving everybody mad." Piles of mushrooms, onion, leek, and turnip filled small bowls ready to be added to the slow cooker. Rosemary, clipped from an abundant bush outside the back door, thyme and oregano were ready. "You can start frying the veal, if you want to help," she said.

Maddie, now her venting had petered out but with the energy of a decrepit slug, nodded as she picked up the wooden spoon. She'd rather be hiding under the duvet upstairs in the guest bedroom but she couldn't tell Caroline that. She just hoped she'd have enough appetite to do the meal justice.

As soon as the *ragout* was cooking, Caroline cajoled Maddie into a walk.

The day was cooling and both put on jackets. "There's a path down to a thirteenth century church. The bell tower is a century younger, fourteenth century. Half an hour's walk or maybe a bit more," Caroline said. "I want to show you the paintings they discovered – hidden, apparently, since Cromwell's men tried to destroy all 'decoration' of churches."

Once in the beech woods, Caroline pointed out several shallow hollows Maddie had not noticed on her first visit there, apparently the remains of pits where flint was mined, flint used to build churches and other buildings centuries ago, including the church to which they were headed.

Slowly Maddie became more interested. The forest was cool, still, and the two of them were alone on their walk. They came out of the woods on to a narrow lane across from an eighteenth century pub, bursting with activity as families spread themselves over picnic tables in the late afternoon sunshine. The two of them crossed the road, avoided the pub to find another ancient footpath that led towards the church.

Once at their destination, the church wall paintings – really more sketches or drawings, but obviously from the thirteenth century because of the fashions depicted – according to the plaque anyway – were indeed fascinating. Maddie knew she was slowly returning to her normal self: interested in history, loving being with her friend Caroline and feeling better now she'd stretched her muscles.

This was a dark period in her life but she could get through it, no matter what was coming. Fingers crossed.

Chapter Twenty-Three

The first thing Maddie did on Monday morning after shooing Jade and Wayne out the door was to make an appointment at the prison where Henry was incarcerated. Visiting hours were that afternoon at two. Her name was on the list of Henry's approved visitors, most likely an oversight on Romania's part in not removing it. Maddie would take advantage.

Henry had aged a decade since Maddie had last seen him. He shuffled to the table where she was sitting, smiling, but looking dreadful. Maddie knew enough not to touch him and also not to comment on his appearance. He slumped in the chair.

"How are you bearing up, Henry?" she asked in a low voice. Other tables were occupied with a variety of people, most of whom were only interested in their own lives, so her low voice was only to emphasise she was aware of privacy issues.

He paused. "Fine. Absolutely fine," he said.

She didn't react to his obvious lie.

"Maybe not quite fine, Mrs Brooks," he said. "Not adjusting quite as well as I'd like." He took a deep breath. "But nothing's happening this end. What about you? Loads going on your end, I gather."

"Oh?"

"The unlovely Ms Carlisle tells me she's now my PO. You are no longer working at the Service."

"Not quite true," she said. "But, you've surmised correctly. I'm having a bit of bother at work and, yes, she's right. I'm not there right now. I'm hoping it can all be sorted…."

His eyes brightened. "But you're here," he said.

"I'm here. You're not forgotten, Henry. Not by me, anyway. But I'm not here officially and there's very little chance I'll be your Probation Officer ever again. So that means I'm here as your friend. In an ordinary private capacity."

A smile slowly spread across his face. "To tell the truth, I'd much rather you were my friend than my Probation Officer," he said.

"How do you find your new PO?" The words were out of her mouth before she could recall them.

"Very different from you, I must say. Ms Carlisle keeps trying to make me confess. As if I'd confess to something I hadn't done." He turned his bright blue eyes on Maddie. "Even if I'd killed that poor child, Carlisle would be the last person I'd ever talk to about it. About anything that mattered."

Maddie found herself smiling then quickly removed her smile.

"I certainly don't blame you, my dear," he said. "I know there's no way I could ever believe you wanted Ms Bloody Carlisle to be your successor."

For a brief moment, she thought he knew about her losing out to Romania for the head of department job, but quickly realised he was talking about himself. She'd been removed and her successor as his PO was Romania.

"The upshot is that I have some time," Maddie said. "I can do my own investigations without supervision or other constraints. Other than obeying the law – the laws of the land and my own personal code of ethics, of course."

His eyes brightened again. "Have you found the lady at the charity shop?"

"Yes and no," she said and brought him up to date about Kathy's travels. "I'm going to double down on tracking her movements starting tomorrow."

"Thank you very much. I appreciate it."

She caught a catch in his voice. The poor man had no support. His wife was gone and anybody he'd known years before he was put into prison had long forgotten him or been turned off by his sex abuser status. And the supposition he had murdered the child from his old school certainly wouldn't be helping. How dreadful to be so utterly alone. Even with her present troubles, she had family and friends like Caroline. And she wasn't in prison.

"I met up with the first victim. Now a young woman." She blurted it out and instantly regretted it. Unprofessional.

"Geneva Hopworth?" He was genuinely surprised. "How is she doing?"

"Well. Grown up. Working. And, moreover, enjoying what she's doing."

"Thank God for that," Henry said. "Why did you want to contact her?"

"Me being nosy."

"Go on, please." He leaned forward.

"You must understand, for her, it was a very long time ago." Maddie hesitated. She was acutely aware discussing this topic with Henry was somewhat improper. Since she'd been put on leave, she'd felt a disconnect from her previous life, a disconnect she continued to feel, emphasised by her weekend away. She was here as a support for him, not as his former PO. She'd better make that clear.

"Look, Henry, even though I'm here as a friend, we'd better keep this conversation private. Between the two of us, just in case I get my job back. Which is not likely." She surprised herself saying this. "Better call me 'Maddie'."

His smile stretched from one ear to the other. "Maddie. I'll try to get used to it."

She smiled back, then let her smile fade. "Can you bear to go back over the Geneva situation once again?" She waited for his answer.

"So you can put Geneva into context?"

"Or so you can freshly remember any details now that you have some distance from it."

He took a deep breath. "Okay. I'll ramble, make an effort to keep relaxed, not trying too hard. Does that sound about right?"

"Absolutely. The less you edit it, the less you fuss over it, maybe the more will come back. We can but try."

He sat back in his chair, closing his eyes. "Cloudy. Cool. Sitting at my desk doing prep work for Monday. Look at my watch. Still got some time before heading over to Susan's place for dinner. Decide to freshen up."

Maddie leaned forward so she could hear better. His voice was a low rumble.

"Glance out at the carpark. Empty except for my car. Everybody was gone."

Maddie grabbed a notepad out of her pocket. She scribbled a question that needed to be answered: 'Any staff normally walk rather than drive to school?'

"Stand outside my classroom and listen," Henry continued. "Silence. Cleaners expected about six. Should be at Susan's by then."

Maddie nodded. New details about the cleaners she hadn't remembered or nobody had mentioned. Also the listening bit. She jotted them down.

"Grab my towel from my locker in the staffroom. Head to the gym. Put my head into the boy's changing room and pull back. Whiffy. Visiting teams' changing rooms were locked as usual. Head to the girls' changing rooms. Stop before going in. Listen. Now my shoes weren't echoing my every step along the corridor, it was utterly silent. I look around. Nobody. Head in." He looked up. Nodded.

Maddie scribbled on her notepad, 'Did not call out before listening?'

"Turn on the lights just inside the door. See two things. A school blazer on one bench and a pair of shoes under another. Decide to drop them off at my locker when I return the towel so I could put them into the 'lost property' box in the morning."

Maddie wrote, 'Blazer to lost prop?' First she'd heard about a blazer.

"When I see those things, I call out. "Anybody here?" I wait. Then repeat my call, which, by the way, echoes around that space. But only silence. So I walk to the shower block, take off my clothes and leave them on the bench just outside."

Maddie remembered Geneva's testimony was that the man coming out of the showers was naked. So seeing clothes on the bench was consistent.

"Have my shower. No soap, just a general rinse-off. But it feels good after the rigours of a typical school day." He paused, his eyes briefly on Maddie's before closing them again. "I turn off the shower and towel off. I take about three steps out of the stall towards the bench and my clothes. I have my damp towel in one hand. I see the girl and let out a … a noise. Maybe a grunt? Maybe a muted scream? Shocked. The girl lets out a screech and turns tail and dashes from the changing rooms. I am horribly embarrassed. I throw on my clothes and rush out the door. Girl long gone. Pause. Hold my breath. Listen. Nothing. Nobody." He opened his eyes again. "It was as if the girl was a mirage." He took another deep breath. "I went back into the changing room and collected my towel and the jacket and shoes. I was disturbed; I was breathing heavily. Annoyed at myself. What a stupid thing to have happened. I hadn't checked carefully enough. The last thing I expected was a child. Maybe the janitor. Maybe a staff member. But it was over an hour since school had closed on a Friday. Everyone had gone." His voice dropped even further. "No sounds. Nobody was there. I even checked Dymock's office. Locked up. The girl had disappeared."

Maddie noticed he'd switched from present tense to past. Was that significant? Up to that point, he was there, in his mind, doing what he said, thinking those things as if re-experiencing it all.

"And?" she asked.

"I walked to my classroom. Collected my coat. Put the jacket and shoes on my desk so I'd be reminded to take them to the lost property box."

"Did it occur to you the girl was after the jacket or shoes?"

"Only much later. Certainly not then. I didn't recognise the child. Did I tell you that? She was not in my home room class nor any I taught."

"The towel?" she reminded him.

"Draped it over my chair to dry. Couldn't be fagged going back to the staffroom. I'd do it Monday morning."

"Okay. Back to what happened…."

"Yes. Well, when I put on my coat, I was feeling okay again. Looking forward to dinner out with friends."

"Your wife not invited?"

He shook his head. "I was baching it. She was visiting her mother up north that week – probably why Susan invited me over as she was more Lucinda's friend than mine. She was trying to help; feeling sorry for me being on my own, most likely. Although that didn't occur to me at the time. I was just pleased to be going out to dinner with people I enjoyed."

"Sorry for interrupting. I promise not to do so again." She smiled at him. "You put on your coat and left the things for the lost property box on top of your desk. And the damp towel on the chair."

"I walked back down the corridor to the side door, the one opening onto the car park. Before I opened the door, I stopped and listened one last time. I thought I heard something that time. Something like, say, a book dropped onto the floor. Muffled. Not a voice. I called out again. Nothing. Told myself it was my imagination and deliberately turned my mind to the upcoming dinner. I had a bottle of wine in the boot, keeping cool. I rescued it and put it in the passenger footwell. Drove to Susan's place. Found a parking spot close by outside her next-door-neighbour's place. Grabbed the wine. Locked up the car with the remote, which worked first time, for once. Headed to the front door. Knocked. Susan answered and ushered me in with a hug. I gave her the wine." He paused. "Any further?"

"Did what had happened in the changing rooms come to mind during the dinner?"

"Not that I recall. I thought of it next when I showered the next morning. Was freshly embarrassed by it. Hoped the child was so startled, she didn't recognise me. A vain hope, as it turned out."

Maddie looked at her questions. "Any of the staff walk to school, or take a bus rather than take their cars?"

"Quite a few, actually, but they're the first out the door so they can catch the bus before the rush hour – hours – get started."

"Walking?"

"Me, usually. And...."

A loud buzzer sounded. All the prisoners rose to their feet.

Maddie said, "I'll be back."

He nodded and turned to walk away with the other prisoners. Maddie watched until he disappeared but he didn't look back.

She had a long drive ahead of her and traffic would be steadily building. But the drive homeward provided a chance to ruminate on what she'd heard. Being careful he was alone in the school would be behaviour she'd expect from a personality such as his. Not calling out at first was not noteworthy. Calling out when going into the girls' changing rooms even if he expected nobody to be there was also consistent with his personality. In fact, the whole episode, including his embarrassed reaction, was consistent.

A falling book. That was his interpretation of the noise he heard at the time. What else makes a sound like that? A closing door?

Chapter Twenty-Four

Maddie had continued to open her work emails although the urgency to do so was fading. She still received some – all the general ones that went out to everybody in the department – and the occasional one from a colleague, mostly asking if she was okay. She hadn't checked her emails since Friday.

Two emails of interest. One from Erin, the psychologist, one from Geneva Hopworth. She opened Erin's. Progress report on Lawrence Reilly, once upon a time, her most despised client. Now of intense interest. Erin said they were cautiously optimistic about the meds. Lawrence said he'd gone an entire evening just watching television. The meant, Maddie knew, an entire evening without his gross and disturbing fantasies. A scrap of hope for the bedevilled man.

Then to Geneva Hopworth's email.

'Hi Mrs Brooks!' the email said. 'Do you still live in Kingston? I've been thinking about what you said about the new murder and the man I accused. Maybe meet at the weekend for a coffee? My treat this time. Best, Geneva.'

It had been sent late on Friday. Maddie cursed the luck. The weekend was well gone, spent with Caroline in Oxfordshire.

She re-read it. 'The man I accused', not 'The man who abused me' or even 'The man convicted of...'. Did the girl have some doubts?

'Hi Geneva,' Maddie replied. 'I have been away for the weekend and only received your invitation for coffee just now and, yes, I still live in Surbiton, just south of Kingston. I would love to meet up again. But I do have access to trains and I also have my own transport, so name a place and I will be there.' She hesitated. Should she suggest after work today? Tomorrow? No, keep it cool. 'Would next weekend be a suitable substitute?' Cool but not cold. Nothing to scare her away.

She looked at how Geneva had signed off and typed 'Best wishes, Madeleine Brooks.' If this came to pass, she resolved to invite Geneva to call her Madeleine. Just a little more formal than 'Maddie' but infinitely better than 'Mrs Brooks'. She pressed 'send'.

Putting aside the temptation to continue working on Henry's case, Maddie set to doing the chores she'd neglected by going away for the weekend. Laundry, putting away a variety of clothes, books, papers and several pairs of shoes and realising she'd need to vacuum. Yet again she found the unmistakable evidence that Jade and/or Wayne ate crisps in front of television.

Next was a clean-up of the kitchen including several meals' worth of dirty dishes and a burnt frying pan with the remains of who-knows-what thoroughly stuck. She put it to soak with fingers crossed.

Enough! Time for some changes.

Okay. They – Jade and Wayne – needed to take regular responsibility for at least one dinner each every week. Neither could cook and it was about time both learned. And it would remove at least one duty from her own shoulders even if she had to teach and supervise for a while. Yes, meals could be planned each Sunday for the week; she'd do five, Wayne and Jade one each. For a start anyway.

She'd do the shopping so the ingredients were all there. No excuses.

She ran up to the computer and produced a form with *Week of* … as the header for the first column filled in with days of the week, and *Maddie, Wayne* and *Jade* along the top of their own columns with empty blocks to fill in with what each planned. It felt assertive and, yes, therapeutic to do it. She printed the form off and placed it prominently on the kitchen bench. Things were going to be different around here. Starting now.

· · • • · • • · · ·

Maddie checked her emails again straight after lunch. Yes! Geneva. She held her breath as she opened it.

'Hi Mrs Brooks! I live in Kingston (with my parents still   ) but I'd rather we didn't meet where my mum could see me. She thinks I've completely erased that whole episode from my memory. I wish! So I'd rather meet elsewhere. How about the Centre Court shopping mall in Wimbledon? There's a café on the upper level in the mall right by the station. Say 9:30 Saturday? (Way too early for any of my mum's friends to be having their elevenses!!!) Best, Geneva.'

Maddie knew the coffee shops in the mall by Wimbledon station. She sent a quick reply agreeing to the time and day and specifying the café. Send.

Perfect.

But when she went outside to wrestle with the worst of the weeds growing around the terrace, she plunged into despair. Wayne. Was he really thinking of having an affair? The woman must be young, given that haircut and the hair dye. An older woman wouldn't care. And had he lost a bit of weight off his incipient beer belly?

She tugged at the weeds with renewed vigour. Once she had a decent pile, she sat back on her heels. Putting the world to rights. A basic part of her existence. Whether it was figuring out what happened to young Geneva or tidying her garden, or, dammit, putting everyone on a schedule, that's what kept her going.

She had to think through how she was going to handle the Wayne problem. Find out more, for sure. Visit him at his studio? They had an unspoken agreement – he didn't show up at the Probation Offices and she didn't drop into his studio. Somehow, such an agreement had evolved over years. Decades. And, now she was thinking about it, she'd had no hand in deciding this should be so.

Who would know what he was up to? She realised she had virtually no relationships with any of his friends or fellow musicians. Wayne socialised during the day. She was aware of that mainly because of the many times a café entry on their credit card bill appeared. Yet, he was always home for dinner. He watched television in the evenings, sometimes with her, sometimes with Jade, but mostly alone while she and Jade did their own things. Jade doing homework and now studying for her exams or texting her friends in her room; Maddie in her home office, lately working, but before that, doing her emails – always several from daughter Olivia – and reading while curled up in her superbly comfy chair in her office with its excellent reading lamp.

She wrestled with a tall weed about to seed. She stood, pulling with all her weight. The weed gave way, snapping off at its base. Maddie cursed. Its roots were intact. She sat down to tackle smaller weeds, those she knew she could handle. But somehow the thought of those viable roots solidly sitting out of sight was disconcerting.

She'd sworn she would never again be in a situation where she lost control. And this instance was too close to home. Far too close.

She was fifteen when her mother had discovered her father was having an affair. Maddie had arrived back home after school to find her mother crying in the sitting room and her father shouting as he packed a bag in their bedroom.

Maddie desperately wanted to interfere, to stop them but didn't know what to do. She knew her mother would hate Maddie seeing her like that. And her father was shouting. Best keep away. She felt her mother's eyes on her back the entire time she dashed up the stairs; she safely arrived at her bedroom without her father seeing her.

She'd flopped on her bed, her fingers in her ears. In spite of that, she could hear her father. "Damnable woman! You can't just let well enough alone, can you? You have to make a big production out of it. But I'll be damned if I can't have a little happiness in my life." And so on.

After her father left, she crept downstairs and made her mother a cup of tea. But when she brought it into the living room, her mother was clutching a tumbler full of scotch.

"You have the tea, dear," her mother had managed to say. "I need something stronger."

Her mother had spiralled down into a depression fuelled by lashings of alcohol leaving Maddie to cope on her own, do most of the housework and cooking and be the only support her mother wanted. She saw her father only rarely after that. He appeared at her wedding, she well remembered, and got maudlin with the drink served. By then he'd remarried, only a year or two later to be involved in another messy divorce.

Maddie didn't care. But she swore she'd never be in a situation where she had no control ever again. And, mostly, that's how she'd lived her life for the next thirty-odd years.

Suddenly Maddie was overwhelmed her own marriage was in jeopardy. Tears, for the first time, filled her eyes. No one was around. No need to pretend. She let them flow. Sitting back on her heels, unseeing eyes fixed on her pile of weeds, gardening gloves on, all alone.

Chapter Twenty-Five

Shirley suggested coffee at their usual place. And here Maddie was yet again, entering the café and spotting Shirley at 'their' table. She waved.

"This is becoming an enjoyable habit," Maddie said as she sat down. "Have you heard from our mutual friend?"

"I have." She waved another letter, replete with closed space handwriting, just like the previous one. "I know now why she's so long in South Africa."

"Sounds like she has had plenty to do." Maddie chucked her jacket, draping it over the back of the chair.

"Yes, I would expect Kathy to fill her days productively no matter where she is, but she had a very practical reason to sojourn in South Africa. And it's all to do with economy."

Maddie smiled. Easy to spot that Shirley was prolonging the moment.

"She got a very good price for her return flight! But she had to wait to take advantage. Such a good excuse to do a thorough job of seeing South Africa and meeting as many of her long-lost relatives as she can."

Maddie thanked the waiter who brought her flat white. "So she found a good deal. And she has the time and energies to take advantage."

"It's winter down there now. So much nicer than if she'd been there during their summertime. Very hot, you know."

Maddie smiled and sipped her coffee. "Did she say when she's coming back?"

"July 27th. So, she's still got six weeks there."

"Did you ask her to call the police here?" Maddie mentally crossed her fingers.

"I did. But she didn't say anything about that. Sorry." Shirley looked abashed.

Maddie kicked herself for not timing her question after Shirley had come down off her high. "I'm sure it's not top of her priorities," she said. "But maybe you can remind her about it when next you write."

"Yes, I'll do that," Shirley said, sipping her coffee. "And I have one more thing to report." She paused for emphasis.

"Go on."

"Nobody called Milhousen was recorded speaking at the Genealogy Society at our last meeting. I specifically asked the secretary but, I have to admit, she doesn't always get every person who asks a question or makes an announcement right. I looked at the minutes. Nothing there. I asked if I could see her scribbles during the meeting. Nothing at the time. But she had a list at the bottom of who attended the meeting. I recognised all the names except for one. A Mr Timmig. Doesn't ring a bell."

Maddie wrote it down. Had Shirley spell it out. "Not Timming? Timmons?"

"Honestly, I don't know how much we can trust Cynthia's spelling, or her hearing for that matter; she's getting on in years. She's been secretary the whole time I've been going to meetings and that's almost a decade."

"Thanks for trying," Maddie said. "I'll see what I can find out." She took a deep breath. "And there's one more thing, Shirley. Do you remember the pile of clothes I took for Henry Macgregor? The clothes he'd left and Kathy had put them under the serving desk?"

"Yes, of course. We met shortly afterwards."

"Do you remember the pile of clothes specifically?" Maddie didn't want to influence Shirley's recollection.

"Yes, for sure."

"Can you remember what was included?"

"But you saw them, Maddie. Didn't you take them into the police?"

"Yes, I did. But I'm wondering if all the clothes were there. Can you recall them?"

"He had a nice navy blue jacket, I do remember that. I think there was a t-shirt and trousers – can't recall the colours but they were both dark coloured. No jersey. No hat. No underwear. No socks or shoes."

Maddie smiled at her. "Exactly what I remember," she said. "No shoes. Did you see him when he was dressed in the suit and tie, the clothes he bought for his luncheon with his daughter?"

"Yes, I guess so. Vaguely." She frowned. "Yes, I must have because Kathy and I had a short discussion about how clothes change a man."

"I saw him later that day," Maddie said. "He was still wearing the outfit he'd bought. We met up after his lunch out. But I cannot remember his shoes. Do you?"

"Sorry. But I do wonder one thing," Shirley said slowly. "When Kathy and I were talking after he'd left, you would think inappropriate shoes would have been in the conversation. You know, 'How lovely that suit looks on him, but too bad about the shoes.' That sort of thing."

Maddie nodded. "Exactly. I didn't notice his shoes either and surely I would have had the same reaction if he had been wearing trainers or even his usual Ecco shoes."

"Ecco shoes? What kind?"

"Soft leather casual shoes. Lace-ups. He has two pairs I've seen over this past year, a black pair and a brown pair. Soft soles, too." She brought her phone onto the table. "I'll google Ecco and see if they have the type of shoes he usually wears. And we can see if they could be worn with a suit and tie without comment or us noticing."

A minute later, she scrolled through the Ecco site until she found what she was looking for, black casual shoes with a price tag of well over £100.00. "There." She passed the phone over to Shirley.

She shook her head. "I can't imagine we'd not notice these shoes if they'd been worn with office gear," she said. "What do you think?"

"I usually pride myself on my powers of observation," Maddie said. "And I agree with you. I think I would have noticed."

They both stared at the image.

"I'll look at their soles." She brought up another photograph. The soles had a small grid pattern, unlike dress shoes and unlike the deep indentations found on all trainers. "Distinctive," she said. "If these are the same. His are over six years old."

"Is it important?"

Maddie shrugged. "I think it could be. Maybe." She grabbed her phone and shut off the image. "They're not trainers, anyway. And I trust myself to have noticed if he had been wearing trainers."

"Me, too," Shirley said.

Chapter Twenty-Six

J ade broke through the throngs of schoolgirls being picked up by their parents. Usually she and Freya walked a little way together, or they would go to one of each other's houses. But Freya was away in New York. New York. Broadway musicals, towering buildings and fashion. Lucky, lucky Freya.

She dawdled along the footpath, not looking forward to another session of studying alone and unaware of pounding footsteps coming up behind her.

"Jade. Wait up," Brody's voice called.

She stopped and glanced around. He looked a right mess. Not only was he wearing his gardening clothes, jeans with ripped knees and bits of grass everywhere, but his hands were red. Bright, blood-like red. She didn't know whether to cower or run. She could hardly breathe.

He grinned at her. "I fixed the bugger."

She noticed red speckles on his hoodie and even his face. "Fixed?" She struggled to get the word out.

He wiped his hands on his trousers. "Bloody paint. Gets over everything."

Relief coursed through Jade's whole being. Paint. Bloody coloured maybe, but paint. "What 'bugger', Brody?" she asked, her voice still faint from the tension.

"Linsey's bloody stepfather, that's who," he said with some enthusiasm. "Do you want to see it?"

Jade stared at him. She could smell the paint now. Definitely not blood. Red paint. "Do I want to?"

"Course you do," he said. "Come on. It's not far. You'll love it."

"What have you done, Brody? Jeez, you're not in more trouble, are you?"

"Probably. But who cares when I'm up for a murder I didn't do."

"They let you go, Brody. You'd be in jail if they thought you'd done it."

He made a face. "That's what Mum says. But I don't trust cops. Do you?"

Jade shrugged. She wasn't going to get into that with him. She just walked half a step behind him, not saying anything.

"He did it. I'm sure."

"Who?"

"That bugger."

There was only one person Brody would call a bugger in this whole scenario. "Linsey's stepfather?"

"He has reasons."

"I know. You told me. But the police know about him and they haven't arrested him."

He frowned. "They should."

Jade shrugged. "My best guess is that he's got a solid alibi. What does he do for a crust?"

"Some sort of salesman, I think." He'd lost his cock-sure look. His steps slowed.

"It was late morning. He was probably at work. And salesmen are with other people at work."

"Other people? They could be lying for him." Stubbornness clouded his speech.

"Yeah, they could." But she knew better. Lying for others was highly unlikely in grownups. Common enough in teenagers, of course. But she could see that sort of blind loyalty fading a bit in herself now. And she was not yet eighteen.

She was becoming increasingly aware Brody wasn't the sharpest tine on the fork. But for all that, she didn't think he was a bad person. And she knew her mother had discounted his guilt in Linsey's murder. Which mattered.

Why had the police not made that clear to him? When people think others have wiped them off the face of the earth, they can find themselves doing stuff they'd not usually do. She glanced at Brody's face. "Come on, Brody. Tell me. What did you do?"

They turned a corner and it was obvious.

"Oh, Brody," she said under her breath.

In the space between the corner of the house and a window, a tall, narrow slot of white render was crudely painted with an elongated stickman. It sported an oversized thingie. An erect thingie, painted in bright, bloodlike red. Under the window was the word 'PERV'. In mirror writing, a large word was painted on the window, its letters dribbling down to the sill. 'SCUM', it read.

"See?" he asked Jade. "You can read 'Scum' from inside." He shot a grin at her.

Over the doorway, he'd written 'KIDDY FIDDLA LIVES HERE'.

"You've certainly made your point," Jade said. "But we'd better get out of here as fast as we can."

Brody frowned.

"If nobody saw you do the deed, it would be crazy to expose yourself now." Oh, ouch. Expose. That was inadvertent.

"Yeah," he said. "But I wanted you to see it. I waited until school was out so I could show you."

"Thanks," she said but quickened her pace. Yeah, thanks for nothing. "I've got to study now, Brody. See you around. And, hey, good luck on not being caught."

"Okay," he said. "You're a good sport, Jade, you know that?"

She smiled and took off, keeping herself under a run, but walking as fast as she could. She hoped he wasn't becoming interested in her. She wouldn't want to create any more angst for the poor guy because, eventually, she'd have to tell him there was no hope of anything happening her end.

Chapter Twenty-Seven

E than dropped by Tuesday morning. "Any chance of a cuppa?" he asked.

Maddie smiled. "Glad you asked. I just happen to have the kettle on," she said. "And I wondered if I'd hear from you." She picked up the paper and waved it at him. On the front page was a photograph of the word 'SCUM' written on a living room window. The headline read, 'House of Murdered Schoolgirl Targeted'.

"You're my conduit into the world of teenage angst."

"Jade didn't mention anything about it but I did see her read that item through to the end this morning. She's usually disdainful of newspapers."

"'Scum' was the least of it," Ethan said. He proceeded to describe to her the other more salacious bits of graffiti decorating the house.

"And you managed to restrict the photographer to that one word?" She passed him a mug of tea. Milk and two sugars, as always.

"He decided he'd not get permission to print any of the other words so prominently displayed. Or the rather graphic diagram." Ethan laughed and lifted his mug of tea in silent salute.

"Awful for the Gainly family."

"Gainly, yes, you're right. Linsey Benton is the stepdaughter," he said. "Besides, it couldn't happen to a nicer guy."

Maddie glanced at him sharply. "You're not impressed with him?"

"Let's just say we're watching him carefully. Not for the murder. His alibi is rock solid. But we did find some rather suggestive diary entries hidden in Linsey's bedroom. Not the kind of evidence that could stand on its own, unfortunately, but evocative, to say the least. It seems as if the graffiti artist knew about the suspicions."

"You're not referring to a young man of our acquaintance?"

"He's awaiting me in the station. I decided to let him sweat a bit. Stop by my friend Maddie's and beg a cuppa from her before hurrying to the station for the interview."

"Meanie," Maddie said. "Drink up. I'd hate to be the cause of more torment to that young fellow." She half meant it.

He emptied his mug and thanked her.

"I'll call you later if anything comes of it," he said at the door.

Half an hour later, he rang.

"Guilty as sin," Ethan said in delight. "We'll get him onto cleaning it up as soon as possible. And he can clean up his hands at the same time. We caught him red-handed, Maddie. Literally."

She grinned. Silly, silly boy.

Chapter Twenty-Eight

Maddie looked up the Saturday trains to Wimbledon. She knew they were frequent because Wimbledon was on the main route to London, but weekends were different. She decided to take an earlier train from Surbiton to avoid any awkwardness of meeting Geneva at Kingston station and having to make small talk until they were in the anonymity of the café.

Maddie caught the 8:48 from Surbiton station and arrived, as planned, just after 9. The shopping mall had opened and she wandered its broad corridors, staring at displays of short skirts and crazy combinations of prints, checks and plains, shaking her head all the while. Somehow, most of the window displays appeared to be appealing to the buyers' market of the very young. How did kids have the money?

Still, she was enjoying herself; she'd tell Caroline about it next time they met. Window shopping was an activity she hadn't indulged in for years. She'd had neither the time nor the inclination.

At 9:30, she entered the café and grabbed a table on the side but where she could see Geneva when she arrived. Which she did almost immediately. Gone were the totteringly-high heeled shoes and the fussy dress and heavy makeup of their last meeting. Instead, Geneva, her shiny brown hair on her shoulders, wearing jeans, trainers and a simple t-shirt, looked to be the teenager she probably still was.

Geneva was frowning. Red blotches on her cheeks. Looking around her with short jerks of her head. Maddie decided to wait for Geneva to find her, rather than waving her over.

Geneva didn't call out as she put in her order, but casually sauntered around the tables until she 'accidently' spotted

Maddie. Maddie, playing the part, gestured for Geneva to join her.

"What a lovely surprise to see you here," Maddie said in loudish tones, as if anyone was listening. So far, the café was sparsely populated.

"Thanks, Mrs Brooks," Geneva breathed as she took her seat. Her hands shook.

"Call me Madeleine," Maddie said. "You're an adult now. My first name is Madeleine."

Geneva's blotches intensified. "Okay, Madeleine. Thanks."

Until their coffees arrived, Maddie gently questioned Geneva about her life, her friends, the music she enjoyed and movies she'd seen. Geneva, her blush faded, became more animated and relaxed, exactly as Maddie had hoped.

But the arrival of the drinks signalled something in Geneva. She took a tiny sip of her coffee and kept her eyes on the surface of her coffee. "Can we keep this confidential? I really don't want my parents to know anything about all this."

Poor kid. Maddie used her most soothing tones. "Unless something is so blatantly dangerous for you or anyone else, I can assure you I will keep our conversation confidential, Geneva. Suits me fine. Suits us both, doesn't it?"

Geneva nodded and took a deep breath. "Something you said last time has been bouncing around in my head, Mrs ... Madeleine. The bit where you said Mr Macgregor could not have murdered little Linsey." She looked up.

"He couldn't. He was buying a new suit for himself and the sales assistant remembers him well. He was actually dressed in the suit when he left the shop and walked to a nearby café, leaving his other clothes in the shop. The sales assistant tucked them away and they were picked up the next day. Macgregor continued to be in public view, having a coffee, then being picked up by his daughter for their fancy lunch together shortly thereafter. He was at that luncheon for several hours. He was arrested by the police not long afterwards."

"Could he have ordered the coffee and left? Gone to the river and killed Linsey, then returned to drink his cold coffee? And the café people didn't notice?" Her voice was almost pleading.

"First, he had no transport and there's no bus service to that spot on the riverbank. Second, he was dressed up for the luncheon. Everything he wore was clean and neat. Nothing was on those clothes, no mud, no soaked trousers, nothing that indicated he had been in the Thames or even on the riverbank. And thirdly, the body of the child was discovered when

Macgregor was in the café or already with his daughter and the medical examiner said she'd been killed only an hour or so earlier, which would have been when he was in the shop buying his new suit."

"Okay. What about the sales assistant? Could she be confused? Maybe the old clothes were wet? That's why he needed to buy the new suit." She was frowning as she said this.

"The clothes were handed into the police as soon as they were collected from the shop the next day. The forensic investigators said they were totally clear of anything suggesting the Thames frontage." Maddie relaxed her muscles to keep her grounded. Geneva had done some good thinking. "You are absolutely right to question every aspect of his alibi. I did too. One other thing, the supervisor of the sales assistant saw him in the shop that morning, as well. I think we can eliminate Macgregor from suspicion."

"Why is he still in prison, then?" Her voice was a bit more assertive.

"Getting out of prison is a massive bureaucratic exercise. It will happen, but things grind slowly in the Corrections system."

"You would know. You're a Probation Officer." Almost aggression.

"Yes," Maddie said, continuing to speak in a calm voice. "Or was, at the time. I'm pleased you want this to be kept between us as I'm letting you know about things nobody else knows other than the police."

"Really?" Geneva said, betraying her youth.

"Really."

"Okay. That makes it clear. And that isn't really what I want to talk to you about. Except it's important that I can trust it wasn't Mr Macgregor this time."

"You're okay with it now?" Maddie looked at her directly, but noticing that Geneva had switched back to 'Mr Macgregor', a teacher's name rather than a criminal's.

"Yeah. Mr Macgregor is in the clear." She played with her spoon, turning it over and over in her hands. "And everyone says whoever killed Linsey also did – you know, the same thing – to her as he did to me. The same thing. Only I lived. And, well, we now know Mr Macgregor couldn't have done it to Linsey." She leaned forward. "Do you think that when they find out who did it to Linsey, they'll look to see if that same guy could have done it to me?"

Maddie's heart pounded. Geneva was considering something that went directly against her previous testimony. "Geneva, will it help if we quietly go over the details leading up to that attack on you? I certainly don't want you to describe what he actually did. We can accept you were attacked and you were only twelve at the time. A disgusting and horrible thing. But can we concentrate for a few minutes on the events before and afterwards?"

"I've been thinking about nothing else since I saw you," she said in a low voice. "I've got to get it out of my brain. I've heard talking about something is good for that. But I haven't anyone I can do that with. Except you, Mrs Brooks."

Maddie didn't correct her. "You discovered you'd left your shoes at school, yes?"

"That's right. My gym shoes. New ones. Mum would kill me if I lost them. But I thought they'd be in my locker."

"And the school was unlocked?"

"The front door was locked. I walked around to the side. When teachers are there, they sometimes leave that door open because it opens on the carpark. Until the last person's car has gone, I guess."

"How many cars were in the carpark?"

"Just one. Mr Macgregor's car."

"Did you know it belonged to him?"

"Not at the time. It was in the papers. He said that car was his."

"That's right," Maddie said. "How about I keep quiet and you can tell it as it occurs to you. I won't interrupt."

Geneva flashed a quick smile. "Thanks, Madeleine. Yeah, that would be great." She turned her head gazing with unfocused eyes at people walking in the mall. Nobody paying a scrap of attention to them. "I tried the side door. It opened. It was creepy. Nobody there. Quiet. I guess because all the windows and doors were shut and nobody was around. I kind of tiptoed to my locker and opened it. It banged open. Really loud in the silence, I can tell you. Scared me. But the stupid shoes weren't there. I stood for a moment and figured the only other place I could have left them would be the girls' changing rooms." She dropped her voice another notch. "I pushed open the door to the changing rooms and spotted my trainers straight away. I headed over to the bench. Then someone came out of the showers. A man." She turned to face Maddie. "No clothes on. Mr Macgregor. He yelped and I ran." She gulped. "Afterwards, like after he'd done it, I ran outside and straight across the carpark and didn't stop until I got home."

Maddie hated interrupting, but the gap wasn't just the rape itself. Maybe Geneva actually didn't remember the events directly before and after the event. Too traumatic. Maddie had to interrupt. "You ran out of the changing rooms? He didn't attack you in there?"

"No. I wanted to hide. Thought I'd be better to disappear than to run down the corridor towards the door. He was an adult. He'd catch me."

She paused again.

"So you hid. Where, Geneva?"

"In the broom cupboard. You know, the cleaner's room."

"How big is that cupboard?"

"Bigger than a normal cupboard. It was walk-in big. Loads of shelves. Machines for polishing the floors, that sort of thing."

"And?"

"He found me. Even though the lights weren't on and it was dark. I was crouched down behind the machines. He grabbed me and choked me. I thought I was going to die. Then he did – you know. The whole time I couldn't breathe. I was gasping. Wanted to throw up. Like totally panicked."

Maddie reached over and put her hand on the back of Geneva's hand. "We don't have to discuss what he did to you. But what about afterwards? He went away leaving you in that room?"

"I ... I guess so. He must have." She looked up at Maddie, her face a picture of distress. "I could hardly breathe, still. I was coughing. I tried to be sick. I couldn't get the ...." She closed her eyes and her voice dropped. "I couldn't get off the ... whatever he'd wrapped around my head. I was freaked out. Trying to breathe, trying to get that thing off my head, trying to see, trying not to be sick." She gulped.

"Something over your head?"

"Something, yeah. I don't know. A cloth. Stretchy. Something that smelled." She brushed tears from her eyes.

"Smelled of what?"

"Sweet. No. Like, you know, that sort of fake pine smell, not that it smells like a Christmas tree or anything. Really strong. Some cleaning fluid probably," Geneva said in obvious distress. "I don't know!"

"Should we stop, Geneva? Is this too much?"

"No!" It came out more loudly than anything else. "No," she said more calmly. "This is the hard part. The part that's been bothering me. How could I know who it was? It was dark where

I hid. And the only person in the school was him. Macgregor. That's why I must have said it was him. It had to be."

Logic. The deduction of a frightened child. "I see why you're unhappy when you follow the logic. Everyone says both crimes on two young girls – you and Linsey – must have been perpetrated by the same individual. One sick man. And Macgregor could not have done both."

"You see why I haven't been able to sleep since I talked to you?" It was almost a wail.

"I understand, Geneva. I absolutely know what you mean." She tightened her hand on Geneva's. "And now you're mistrusting you were correct in identifying Mr Macgregor."

"It was him in the shower. I know it was."

"Yes, it was him. He said he was there. He saw you. But in the cupboard when the man disappeared and you had to get whatever it was off your head – something smelly?"

"I honestly don't know what it was. Probably a cleaning cloth. It was stretchy, I remember that. Pulled down like a balaclava over everything but my … my mouth. He said we were going to play a game. A fun game." She took a shuddering breath. "He said, 'What fun!' like it was fun." Not. Not one speck."

Maddie quickly moved on. "What else did he say?"

"Nothing, Madeleine. Nothing. Just grunted. Not that I could hear much." Geneva paused. "His hands were over my ears for … when … you know. That produced a loud noise – you know the kind of noise. When he left, all I heard was him going out."

"Going out? Him running away?"

"No. Just the door shutting."

"The cupboard door."

"Yeah. I was panicked he'd locked me in. But he hadn't. I waited for ages before I poked my head out. Then headed for the outside door and ran home."

"Mr Macgregor's testimony was that he dressed and looked for you but you'd long gone. He said he went back to his classroom to leave the shoes and blazer he found in the changing rooms to take to the lost property in the morning and then left by the side door by the gym. I gather it was a door with a push handle so anyone could leave but not re-enter."

"That's right. Same door as me."

"He said he then got into his car and drove off."

Geneva shook her head. "Something else I remember. His car was gone."

"From the carpark?"

"Yeah. It was empty."

Maddie didn't comment. It depended on how long she sat in the cleaner's cupboard whether or not Henry had time to leave. But with his car gone.... "No other sounds? Just the closing of that door?"

"Not that I remember. Actually, I'm amazed how much I remember, Madeleine. Way too much, in fact."

"Have you seen a trauma therapist, Geneva?"

"A horrible lady who smelled of talcum powder. She was trying to make me talk but I was a stubborn kid, way back then." She grinned at Maddie. The first smile in far too long.

Maddie smiled back but her mind was running at breakneck speed. "How will you be after our coffee? I'm not a therapist and I don't know what's best now we both know each other's thoughts."

"I'm glad we met up, Madeleine. Do I have to talk to the police?"

"I'm not altogether sure the timing is right." She hated that Geneva might feel brushed off. "The sales assistant needs to make her statement to the police first, I would think. Then your statement will be seen in the correct light."

"Will you know when that is?"

"Yes, and the first thing I'll do is to invite you for another coffee and you can practice what you'll say with me. Okay?"

Geneva's face cleared. "Perfect." She got up. "I'm supposed to be buying a hoodie that's on sale. I better go and choose one so I can get home before Mum goes ballistic."

As she watched the young woman set off on her mission, Maddie thought Geneva's mother must be still suffering all these years later. Or why else would she need to know what her almost twenty-year old daughter was doing on a Saturday morning?

Maddie headed back to the train station. She'd just missed a train to Surbiton, so found a bench to sit on. A bit of time to figure out the timing, putting together both what Henry had told her with what Geneva had now remembered.

It started with Henry believing he was alone in the school. But the side door was open. (Presumably Geneva had not yet arrived at the school.)

He used a shower off the girls' changing room.

Geneva entered the school and immediately checked her locker – no shoes – before entering the changing room. She spotted her shoes and crossed to the bench well inside the room.

Henry had finished his shower before Geneva got there (she did not mention the sound of a shower and was surprised by Henry's appearance from the shower room). He must have been silently towelling off. He then walked naked into the changing room and was surprised by Geneva.

She ran out of the changing room into the corridor. Henry did not. He presumably did not rush after her because of his naked state, so dressed first.

While he was dressing, Geneva hid in the broom cupboard.

The perpetrator followed her. Put a stretchy, smelly tube of cloth over Geneva's head.

Orally raped her. (How long would that take? The very question was nauseating.)

Meanwhile, Henry, now fully dressed, including shoes, came out of the changing rooms and thought the child long gone.

He walked to his classroom then retraced his steps to get to his car. He hesitated a moment by the outside door near the changing rooms before leaving the building. That's when he heard a book drop (or a door close?). Followed by silence. (Was the noise made by Geneva? She mentioned nothing about a noise. And it was not her closing the door of the broom cupboard because Henry would have seen her. Thus the noise was made by either the perpetrator or something outside of the school. Of course, it could have occurred during the rape. Geneva would not have heard anything with his hands over her ears and the perpetrator's attention would have been elsewhere, to say the least.)

At one moment, Geneva was in the broom cupboard, Henry at the side door to the outside and the perpetrator either with Geneva or somewhere close by.

Henry left by the side door and drove off to dinner with friends.

Geneva, after the rape, hid for some time. No way to estimate.

But when Geneva left, she noticed Henry's car had gone.

It could all fit, although with glaring holes in the timing.

On the train back, Maddie switched to her other worry. Kathy. When would she come back? And, importantly, who was the man who provided her with tickets to South Africa? That was a question that should be answered.

Maddie leaned her head back on the seat, letting the view out the window pass by without her noticing. Geneva and what she went through. Her recent ruminations about what happened. Her doubts.

So much depended upon Kathy.

Chapter Twenty-Nine

M addie collapsed in front of her computer and made herself
look through her emails. She wrote a quick reply to Olivia
claiming she was having a Rest and Recreation day. Invited
Olivia and her family for Sunday lunch, feeling guilty they were
taking so little of her thinking time. Sent the same message by
text. Glanced at the book she'd just finished which was sitting on
the side table next to her chair. She needed to get it back to the
library. Sighed.

She called up YouTube on the laptop and searched on 'house
renovation'. She loved television shows that showed some
genius who took a tired house and, with a bit of creative magic,
transformed it into something beautiful or practical or, often,
both.

She chose a programme she had never seen, clicked on it,
paused it, brought her comfy chair to the desk, repositioned the
screen of her laptop and settled in to watch a house
transformation in sunny Australia. A home-handyman bought an
unlovely shed-like cottage in a clearing in an open woods. He
fixed it up so it looked new and inviting. Now, if it had been her,
she would have done things a little differently. Maybe making
the south, no, north window much bigger letting the light flood
inside. Or maybe building a small patio outside the back door
dressed with a barbecue and an outdoor eating area with an
umbrella. Not costly, but inviting potential buyers to imagine
themselves there.

In the programme, the handyman eventually sold it as a
countryside retreat for almost double the original investment.
Oh, how she'd love to be involved somehow. Not that she had
the skills to do renos herself, but what fun to advise, then
influence owners who wanted to change the market value with

some innovative renovations. How could she do it? Maybe become the person who would eventually sell it, making money for the owner and a fat commission for herself?

What training could a middle-aged woman take to learn how to sell houses? She searched on Google and found lots of sites offering courses. Some very expensive, some dirt cheap.

Interesting.

She shut her eyes and imagined being in such a life. Dealing with tired and broken things, not tired and broken people. Living somewhere else. Not the city, not the suburbs, but in a town or, better yet, a village. Getting to know her neighbours. Working her own hours. Living the seasons rather than noticing the weather only when it interfered. Having people over for dinner. Growing her own vegetables. Putting herself first. Her dream.

An impossible dream.

When she woke up, she was horrified to see the afternoon had gone. She had not even thought about dinner. She rushed downstairs to see her new weekly schedule sitting where she'd left it, prominently supported by the salt shaker and pepper grinder on the kitchen table. It gave her pause. Why should she be fussing about not having the meal on the table? Why was it always her responsibility?

No time for change like the present.

With a little more energy since she'd had her nap, she reached into the freezer and pulled out some sausages. She put them under warm water to defrost. She pulled lettuce, tomatoes and her homemade mayonnaise from the fridge. She grabbed bread rolls left over from mid-week. A bit stale but she knew the trick. She put them beside the sink and turned on the oven. When Wayne came in, she'd get him to light the barbecue and get on with the dinner. Her contribution would be to pass the rolls quickly under the running tap and put them immediately in the oven. By the time the sausages were cooked and the salad made, her rolls would be rejuvenated, warm and crusty.

Under 'Saturday' on the schedule in Wayne's column, she put 'BBB sausages, salad and rolls'. She went upstairs to start another house programme on YouTube.

It didn't quite go according to plan.

Jade arrived home with Freya after shopping for more t-shirts. Her excuse was that she could wear what she wanted – she and Freya were going to ceremonially burn their school uniforms once exams were finished – when she became a university student. If she became a university student with the little swot she was doing. Maddie sighed.

Wayne, coming from his usual Saturday jam session with his musical pals, arrived shortly before six.

"What's for dinner?" he asked before he was into the kitchen.

"Your turn," Maddie called from upstairs in her home office.

"Excuse me?"

"We're going to share the housework and the cooking from now on," she called.

"A bit menopausal, are we?"

She didn't deign to answer that one. And she didn't rush downstairs although she could feel her heartbeat increase in tempo. She hated confrontations with Wayne. She'd been avoiding them for decades.

She heard Jade and Freya follow Wayne into the kitchen. When curiosity finally drove her downstairs, she found the girls cutting up the salad things and Wayne chatting to them from the barbecue.

"Dad said Freya could stay. She's off to New York tomorrow. That okay?"

"His dinner. His say," she said. "But you don't have to make Freya work. Especially if she'll have to pack and do stuff at home."

"Course she has to," Wayne said from just outside.

The girls grinned.

"When I'm at Freya's, we always do the veggies, don't we, Freya?"

"And Dad does the meat. Sometimes barbecuing, sometimes, you know, on the cooktop or in the oven."

"He does the cooking?" Maddie asked as she dampened the rolls.

"Mostly. Sometimes Mum but never at the weekend. I help him, though. Both of us do when Jade is over."

"I'll freshen the rolls," Maddie said, putting the rolls into the hot oven.

If only it could always be like this.

After doing the dishes (small changes, she reminded herself, no rush), in a blast of enthusiasm, she ran upstairs to sign up for an internet estate agent course. When she was asked for the credit card payment, she laughed at herself. What on earth was she doing? That's when it all piled back on her: trouble at work, a big question mark over her marriage and her frustration at Henry's continued incarceration. She had to do something but signing up for an internet course wasn't it. Get through the weekend then on Monday, she'd drop in on Ethan with the relevant material from her talk with Geneva fresh in her mind.

He probably wouldn't mind sharing information about an old solved case. Maybe.

She closed the page.

Chapter Thirty

Jade's phone rang. Donald Dymock's phone. Must be Freya using her dad's phone. She was back in the States, not due back for another couple of weeks for her final final exam. If she came back, that is.

"Hey, Freya!" she said into the phone. "You ringing from New York?"

"Sorry, Jade, not Freya. It's Donald and I'm here in England. I've got something to ask. You okay to talk?" He sounded a bit breathless, rushing his words.

"No prob, Donald. How can I help?"

"Freya has asked me to bring over her warm-weather clothes. Gave me a huge list. Any chance you know her clothes better than me?"

Jade smiled. "Probably. Yeah, I'd know what she was talking about, anyway." More than any father would, that's for sure. She thought of her own father who, most likely, wouldn't be able to identify a single item of her clothes.

"Any chance you can pop over now? I'm due to catch a plane later today."

Jade looked at her history books spread over her room. Any excuse. "Yeah, I can come." She paused, hoping he'd say he'd come fetch her, but he didn't. "I'll bike over. Be there in fifteen minutes or so."

"You're a poppet, Jade. See you shortly."

She clicked off her phone and hastily changed into shorts and a sleeveless t-shirt. It was hot out. Biking over to the Dymocks was much better, much, much better than sweltering in her room going over and over stuff. Besides, she could put her ear buds in and review the recordings she'd made earlier. Studying while cycling. See where she faltered then concentrate on that when she got back home. It could work.

Jade took the more direct route rather than the longer but more scenic tow path route. She'd remembered to pull on a hat, too. Reviewing three chapters of their history text later, not much over her estimated fifteen minutes, she leaned her bike against the low wall in front of the Dymocks' house. She knocked.

"There you are," Donald said. "I really appreciate this, Jade."

She grinned at him. He was such a lovely dad. Freya didn't appreciate him as much as she did. He was sort of a second father to her, she'd always thought.

Jade followed Donald up to Freya's room. He handed her the list.

"You figure out what she wants and I'll pack them into the case," he said. "First, three hoodies? She owns some hoodies?"

Jade laughed and opened up the wardrobe. "Which colours?"

"Um, black, navy blue and denim." He looked up. "Denim is a fabric, not a colour."

"It's a colour, Donald. This colour." She grabbed a dull blue marl hoodie and gave it to him, then the other two.

"Okay. Now two swimming cozzies."

"Got them," Jade said, with two bikinis in her hand.

"She doesn't say which two."

"Her bikinis, for sure."

"Maybe I'd better take all three," Donald said. "They're little enough to pack."

"No need. She'd want the two bikinis. Not the swim squad one piece. It's too small for her anyhow."

"Okay. Now, jeans – blue, black and cut-offs."

Jade opened the bottom drawer of the chest of drawers. "These are her favourites," she said as she grabbed two pairs of jeans, leaving several others. She opened the shorts drawer and pulled out the cut-offs.

And so they worked through the list. It became hotter and hotter as the westerly sunshine flooded the bedroom.

"What a wonderful friend you are," Donald said. "And such a pretty one, too." He smiled at her.

She could feel herself redden. Wonderful, yes. Pretty, not so much. But she felt hugely complimented that such a good looking teacher would say she was pretty, even if it had been just Freya's father. What a great dad Donald was. She wished her dad would say nice things to her about something. Anything.

"That's it, Jade. Thank you so very much. Hey, how about a little dip in our pool to cool off before biking home? You deserve it."

Jade hesitated.

"Look, wear the cozzie Freya didn't want. Maybe too small for her but not for you."

"Just a quick dip, thanks, Donald. Yeah, the swim squad one should fit me. Not that I'd want to be seen in it." She laughed and he laughed, too.

After he left, she quickly shed her clothes and pulled on the ugly swimming costume. For someone with such small boobs, she would never have picked a costume that squished her to nothing like this one did. But she was hot and a swim would be just the thing. She wrapped a towel she found in the bathroom around her and headed to the back garden.

To her surprise, Donald was in the pool.

"Come on in! The water's lovely," he said.

She dropped the towel at the water's edge and dived in. The pool was so small, her hands touched the other side before she popped up her head.

"Come down to this end," he called.

She did, basking in being the centre of his attention.

"Race you," Donald said with some glee. "One, two, three!"

They both powered down the pool to the opposite end. His hand brushed against her body. Twice. She kicked to put a bit of space between them.

"I won!" he said. "Try again?"

She nodded, surprised at his playfulness, and was ready for his count to three this time.

They splashed to the other end of the pool, ending up tangled together as they hit the edge of the pool. Jade felt herself being pushed beneath the surface. She flailed to get out from under, her hand inadvertently contacting Donald's body.

"Sorry," Jade said automatically as she surfaced. Appalled. Her arm had slid down his front, her hand touching ... no. Couldn't be. He was Freya's father. But he had been hard. Like a boy on the dance floor.

Donald's face was only inches from hers. He reached out, put his arms around her and they both sank. Spluttering, they surfaced and Donald grinned at her. "Isn't this fun!"

Shit.

He wrapped his arms around her tighter this time and they both sank again. Jade could feel him pushed against her. He must not care. Want her to know.

"Please, Donald," she gasped when they rose to the surface and before he pulled her down under the water once more. She struggled. His face too close to hers, his hands all over her. She finally got one leg up, her foot on the wall of the pool, her knee bent. She'd only have one shot if this was going to work. As Donald moved into her spread legs, she pushed against the pool wall with all her might and shot out of his arms like toothpaste from a tube.

She scrambled out of the pool, grabbed the towel and ran like a gazelle. She hopped on her bike and took off as fast as she could go. She glanced back at the house. She spotted him as she was turning the corner. Would he come after her? Her heart pounded. He had a car. He could be onto her in moments.

She was headed towards the Thames – the towpath – but she wouldn't take a direct route. It couldn't be the usual way. She wove her way through back streets, looking behind her every time she turned a corner. She needed to get close enough to recognise a tiny footpath which led over the grass and down to the towpath. On her bike, she'd be able to whizz down to the level of the river. Where no cars were allowed.

She raced along yet another street, a cross street and another suburban street to get ever closer to the river. Finally, at full tilt, she crossed the street parallel to the water, jumping over the edging of the road to the tiny winding footpath she and Freya used to get them down to the towpath and she was soon flying down the slope. She screeched to a stop on the path. Glanced back up the slope. No Donald.

She wrapped the towel more securely around her middle and slowly pedalled along, catching up to a group, a couple of kids on little bikes cycling ahead of two women. She slowed. Had to catch her breath.

"Have you had a swim in the Thames?" one of the women asked, disbelieving but curious.

"Not a chance. Just a friend's swimming pool," Jade answered with a smile she forced onto her face. "I've been cycling flat out. Time to take it easy." She passed the two children to distance herself slightly but kept a steady distance just ahead of them. She glanced up at the top of the rise. Still no Donald. She was not in a hurry now. Besides, safely in numbers.

And it gave her time to think. Could she be misinterpreting? But a guy's hard-on is a guy's hard-on. Every girl knew what it felt like. Even every virgin. Not that she was still virginal, but she'd known what it felt like to be clutched tightly on the dance floor from the time she was thirteen or so. She'd had one hand or the other pushed downward too often not to be totally sure what she'd felt.

Donald. The thought made her want to puke.

At the spot she had to leave the towpath, she sped up again, constantly checking behind her for Donald's car. She got a second wind. Only about four minutes to go.

Chapter Thirty-One

Maddie looked over at David Player. They were seated in the corridor outside Bettina Rossmore's office on two chairs obviously put there for the purpose.

"Same rules as before, Madeleine. I won't answer any questions put to you by either Bettina or Romania. I will only contribute if you're getting into hot water within my area – the most likely will be to request some time alone with you. Of course in the meeting, you can ask me anything or defer to me. You're in charge."

Maddie nodded. She liked how he made it so clear she was at the helm. Enabling. For all his youth, David Player knew what he was doing.

A long ten minutes later, they were ushered into the office. Bettina was in one easy chair and Romania in a second placed in front of a coffee table. David and Maddie took the couch opposite. Maddie didn't even try to return Bettina's smile. The arrangement presumably was to give the impression of a friendly-friendly conversation, but it really looked like a case of 'us against them'. It would have been better if they'd been spaced evenly around a table. She introduced David to Romania.

"Surely this doesn't involve the union," Romania said to Bettina.

"It's Madeleine's right to have it present at any of these meetings. This young man has been a help already." She turned to David. "Welcome, Mr Player."

"David," he said pleasantly.

Bettina sat forward. "I've gone over and over all the personnel regulations for our service, both with my supervisor and Human Relations. I have been appointed the Deciding Officer in this case," she said in a slightly louder voice. "To let you know in the interests of transparency, Ms Carlisle – Romania – is currently being instructed in the skills of managerial supervision as she is new to this role. The regulations are quite clear what happens next. In instances like this, we have a protocol that must be followed." She flicked her eyes from one to the other.

Maddie was mollified although still wary. So far, it didn't seem that Bettina was favouring Romania. Nor her either, of course. But Romania undergoing management training was good. Otherwise, neutral was good. Probably good.

"Madeleine," Bettina said, turning to her, "you will be put on supervision for a four month period starting on your return to work. Romania will hold a supervisory meeting with you on a weekly basis setting out goals for the next week and going over the goals from the previous week."

Maddie felt herself flush. Supervision?

"Romania will then meet with me," Bettina said, "and we will go over each meeting in some detail, including how you are doing and what is appropriate for the next set of goals."

Maddie frowned, started to speak.

Bettina held up a hand. "We will discuss it all once I've outlined the entire package."

Maddie sat back, controlling her breathing. Once a week with Romania? Then it hit her. Those last few weeks of work, she had been called into far more supervisory meetings than one a week. This would be a reduction. And the weekly supervision meeting would be analysed by Bettina each time.

"I presume you'll have some sort of contact with Mr … with David each week as well. Is that so, David?"

"I'm willing to comply with any and all regulations," he said a tad stiffly.

"I'm happy to have David involved," Maddie said with a quick glance at him. "I presume if there is anything to complain about, he'll advise me to … to what, David?"

"To contact the Deciding Officer, who is Bettina in this case."

Bettina beamed, clasping her hands in front of her. "We can get through this. We can learn to work together." She turned to Maddie. "You wanted to comment?"

"Just to go over it all, thanks. So, Romania and I have a meeting to set goals for the week. The next week, we go over how I have achieved those goals and amend them for the coming week. That's it?"

"Essentially." She turned to Romania. "You have a comment?"

"Are you saying that I have a weekly meeting with you as well? That's a lot of meeting time to squeeze into my busy schedule. Two meetings about Madeleine's performance. As well as the managerial training."

"Two meetings to discuss both your performance and Madeleine's," Bettina said.

It was Romania's turn to flush.

"If this meeting is concluded, I'd like a private word," Romania said to Bettina.

"Fine," Bettina said as she nodded to David and Maddie with a small tight smile. They walked out, closing the door behind them.

Sounds of a rising voice could be heard through the closed door. They glanced at each other.

"Hey," David said and gave Maddie a high five.

Chapter Thirty-Two

Maddie was barely home from the Probation Service hearing when she heard a bicycle crash down onto the back steps.

"Oh, there you are," Maddie said when Jade rushed in through the kitchen door. "I've been ringing you."

Jade took one horrified glance at her mother and raced upstairs, the towel dropping to the floor revealing what she was wearing. Maddie, concerned at the look on her daughter's face, and noticing her odd attire, walked up after her. She picked up the damp towel and stood for a moment at the door to Jade's room, looking in. Jade was now curled in the foetal potion on her bed, still clad in the unusual swimsuit. Maddie felt her mouth go dry. What had happened? She walked in and put the towel – not one of theirs – on the end of Jade's bed.

"Something's wrong, isn't it, Jade? Very wrong." She held her breath. Jade, as a teenager, had not been forthcoming. Yet, when she was little, she'd been talkative and continually open.

At first Jade didn't move. She slowly nodded and took a deep and shuddering breath.

Maddie sat on the edge of the bed and reached over to stroke Jade's back.

"Borrowed swimming costume, borrowed towel. And you're upset." Maddie didn't dare push too hard. "I'll go put the kettle on. Stay here. I'll bring it up."

She was terrified she'd destroy any potential of meeting Jade half way about whatever had frightened her so badly. As she waited for the kettle to boil, the tea things ready when it did, Maddie ran through the possibilities. Not an argument with Freya – she was in New York. No boyfriend at the moment and none of the signs of Jade having a crush on some boy either.

Certainly nothing about school – her exams were going well and her studying, erratic and too dependent upon last minute cramming, was producing results, as usual. And the strange swimming costume? Jade, and all of her friends, had worn nothing but bikinis for years.

Who had a pool? The Hampton Pool was biking distance taking the Bushy Park route, but Jade would not have been seen dead in that costume at a public pool. Her friend Kim out in Esher had a pool, but that was not within biking distance. Freya had a pool. But she was ... oh. Maybe she'd returned unexpectedly. Didn't Freya swim with the school team a couple of years ago?

Maddie made their mugs of tea and went back upstairs. Jade had not moved. She put the mugs on the bedside table and once again perched on the side of her daughter's bed. She kept her voice soft. "Freya's old swimming costume from the swim team, right? You've been over there?"

Jade turned an anguished face to her mother and reached for a hug.

With huge relief, Maddie gathered Jade into her arms and stoked her hair. It had been a long time. The last time Jade had hugged her like this was years ago. "Tell me," she murmured into Jade's ear.

"Donald," Jade whispered.

Maddie stifled a gasp.

Jade proceeded to tell her increasingly dismayed mother what had happened. "I thought I was going to drown," she wailed. "And he was, like hot ... for me!" She sobbed in her mother's arms.

Jade, who'd always thought Donald was an ideal dad.

Jade, who looked years younger than her age.

Donald, pushing someone under water and saying it was fun.

Donald, an aroused, muscular man who looked like a farmer from the veldt....

Maddie was frightened for her daughter. Extremely frightened. And increasingly angry.

Chapter Thirty-Three

Maddie helped her daughter shower and wrapped her in a big fluffy towel afterwards. Something about cleansing yourself. Being clean. Being supported. She grabbed jeans and a t-shirt for Jade to wear, back to Goth black, but Maddie couldn't find anything else.

Jade wanted her phone back, needed it. She'd prepared a series of recordings she was using for her exam preparation and she was adamant they had to go and get it. And pick up the clothes she worn earlier.

She broke down into tears at her own internal conflict. "I want to get them. But I don't want to see Donald again. I can't see him again," she said to her mother in some distress. "I just can't. Don't make me, Mum."

"I have no intension of making you, darling girl. Should I go to collect them? Or would that make it worse?"

"No. No, you don't have to. Really." She sat up, pushing her hair out of her eyes just like she used to do when a small child. "I'll do it. But maybe you could give me a ride."

"Of course," Maddie murmured, well aware of her role as just being there. "Let's plan it out. All the 'what ifs'."

Jade nodded. "You drive me. You park outside the door. Even if someone else is there, you stay close, okay?"

"Double park if necessary. Agreed."

They made a plan. Maddie would accompany Jade to the door. She'd engage Donald in conversation. As if she had not been told what had happened between them earlier. Jade would hurry upstairs and grab her gear. If Donald insisted on going upstairs with her, Maddie would tag along as well. It was as good a plan as any.

The last thing Maddie wanted to do was to have to see Donald Dymock. But needs must and that was all there was to it. She had no intention of letting Jade go alone.

As Jade dressed, Maddie could see she was near tears several times. Not her usual self. Obviously conflicted. She dithered; fussed with her hair; couldn't find her favourite shoes. Maddie didn't want to push her, but if they wanted to collect the phone and clothes, they had to do it soon. After all, Donald had told Jade he was off to New York today.

"Come on, darling. There's a certain safety in being a twosome," Maddie said. "I won't leave you."

They set out to drive the short distance to the Dymock house, both now silent.

As they drove up, they spotted Donald in front of his house busy fitting several suitcases into his boot. He had not yet left but it looked as if he was close to doing so.

Maddie slowed the car as she drew her car up alongside his. She lowered her window. "Hello, Donald. Glad we caught you."

Donald looked momentarily startled, then relaxed into his usual smile.

"Jade's left some things here. She needs them, if that's all right." Maddie squirmed at her own middle-class politeness.

"Ah, Madeleine." He gave a self-assured smile. "I'm just off to New York. And a plane waits for no man, at least, no ordinary man." He smiled at Jade. "Your clothes are still upstairs. I'll pop up to get them."

"She can do it, Donald." Maddie smiled but she knew her smile was steely.

"I'll just be a minute." Jade managed a wobbly smile, opened the car door and scooted towards the house.

"Tell me, Donald, what are your plans for the rest of the summer? Your term wouldn't start until September, I presume?" She prattled on, hoping Jade would grab her things and rescue her. Trying to control her anger at this man. This man she had trusted.

Donald answered her in desultory tones, also watching for Jade's reappearance. He obviously felt as awkward as Maddie, if not more so. Definitely he should feel more awkward given what had transpired.

Maddie stayed double parked with the engine purring. Donald couldn't drive away until she did and she was not going to give this muscular man an opportunity to do anything untoward. She decided to play it cool and they switched topics just to keep up the pretence of being sort of friends. The barbecue, the people there and his plans for his new job in New York.

Time passed. And Maddie was rapidly running out of topics. Donald was looking increasingly twitchy.

Still no Jade.

· · · ● ● · ● ● · · ·

Jade had grabbed her clothes from Freya's room immediately. Where was her phone? She remembered putting it on the bed beside her clothes. Had it dropped onto the floor? She searched in the vicinity and also under the bed in case she'd inadvertently kicked it there.

But no. Where was it? She stood, her clothes in one hand, her eyes searching every surface. She put the clothes back onto the bed and sorted through all pockets and rummaged through her backpack. No phone anywhere.

Jade wandered out into the corridor and stood listening. Thinking. She could barely hear murmuring voices through the open door below.

The phone wasn't where she left it. Definitely. So, where would he have put it? She cautiously opened a door. A cupboard for clean laundry, extra bedding and other stuff. She closed it and walked to the door opposite. A bedroom. A large bedroom. She spotted a carry-on bag. It had several outside pockets. Would he? She reached inside first one then a second pocket. Yes. Two mobile phones. She made a quick decision.

"Jade?" Her mother's voice. Not outside. Coming up the stairs.

Jade scurried out of the room and into Freya's bedroom, shoving the phones to the bottom of her bag. She jammed her clothes on top and swung the backpack in place.

"Ready to go?" her mother asked.

Jade didn't reply, just pushed past her mother and headed down the stairs as Donald came out of his bedroom, his carry-on bag in one hand.

"Stop." Donald said in his teacher's voice bellow. His voice quietened. "I believe you have something of mine."

Now at the half way point, Jade stopped and glanced up.

Her mother was at the top of the stairs, Donald in the corridor, coming up behind her. "What?" Jade asked. Things were deteriorating.

"Give it back. It's not yours."

Still at the top of the stairs, Maddie half turned to Donald. "What are you talking about?"

Jade saw his chest heaving. Emotion poured out of him. Anger.

"She knows what."

Jade turned a defiant face towards him. Her mother must have recognised what was going on inside her. She gave a slight shake of her head. But no way was Jade going to give up on this. Never. This was a stand-off and she could run faster than he could. She'd already proved it.

"I said, give it back. Put it down on the stairs."

Her mother frowned. "For heaven's sake, what are you two talking about?"

At that point, Donald grabbed Maddie from behind, his thick forearm around her throat, choking her. "Put it down, Jade, and nobody will get hurt."

· · • • • • • • · ·

Maddie struggled, panicking. She couldn't breathe. Donald was cutting off her air supply. She arched her back, instinctively grabbing his arm, trying to loosen it so she could breathe. He shifted slightly and that allowed her to grab half a breath.

"I said, put it down. Now." His voice was too loud, her ears too close for the volume. "You don't want your mother hurt, do you, little Jade?" He glanced over the balustrade to the floor below. "That's a stone floor down there. Pure and hard. Look at it."

Donald pushed Maddie against the railing of the bannister. She knew that floor and she felt faint with terror. Cold and dark. Right below where they stood. Fashionable slate. She'd noticed it the first time she'd been in the house.

Jade said nothing. Maddie knew Jade understood the threat. She would think he wouldn't dare. Think it was intimidation with no substance behind it. Maddie knew better. Donald Dymock was a murderer. Her heart thumped inside her chest; she could feel her face reddening with lack of blood flow. She had to do something. Or she'd black out.

"You'll be responsible. It's up to you. Well, Jade?" He pushed Maddie onto the railing again, tightening then loosening his arm for a second or two. Cat and mouse. But it allowed her to grab half a lungful this time.

What could she do? What? Think.

First, calm down.

He straightened. Tightened his hold on her and she fought panic again.

Think.

She'd had been taught plenty of self-defence courses over the years. Never had to use the techniques. Rusty. Out of practice.

Think.

"I can upend her in two seconds. A floor like that will do the rest." He shifted again. "You know what hitting a slate floor does to a head? It explodes, Jade. Picture those brains splattered all over the walls. You want that, Jade?"

Maddie's training came surging back: First attack the weak points.

Eyes.

No go. Her arms could hardly move and she could reach nowhere near his eyes.

Groin.

Also no. She was facing away so she couldn't knee him where it hurts.

His thick thighs were pushing against her again. She could no longer breathe. She could feel giddiness coming and going. She didn't have much time.

What did that last self-defence guru say? 'Never be a victim.'

Too late.

No, not too late. She was not a victim. Never.

'Hit hard.' Can't with that arm around her throat. Donald shifted a bit again and she got a little air out, some in. Playing with her. Two stories here – number one was Jade. Number two was Maddie's air supply.

'Only use techniques your muscles remember.' The only thing left is, what muscles?

Oh.

The roll. Yes, the roll.

Energy surged back through her body. Did her muscles remember? They'd better.

She'd practised and practised it way back when.

Jade? Could she get out of the way? She had to trust she would.

Donald straightened again. Adjusted his forearm. Maddie grabbed a little air.

Now or never.

She suddenly dug her fingers hard into Donald's forearm. He jerked back. Not much but enough to get another breath. Her thoughts swirled: squat, shove the hips back and pull. All at once. Squat, hips back and pull with all her might.

She squatted, shoving her bottom hard into his groin and at the same time she put her whole weight onto his arm to roll him over her head.

Yes!

Up and over he went, bumping on his back down the stairs. Screaming, his arms flailing. Past Jade who scrambled out of the way.

Got him!

"Let's go," she yelled at Jade who nimbly jumped over her groaning tormentor, closely followed by her mother. They raced out the door to the car. Maddie had hastily turned off the engine when Donald had decided to investigate why Jade was taking so much time. And she'd left the car double-parked. No way would she have allowed him alone with her daughter.

Now they were at the car.

In it.

Engine started and she pulled away.

"Have a good trip, Donald. Tada," Maddie called out as they drove off, as if Donald could hear. "Give my love to Sharon and Freya."

Jade glanced at her mother and grinned.

That did it.

"Bumpity, bump, bump," Maddie squealed.

"Ooooow," Jade cried, grabbing her head just as Donald had done.

They broke down in uncontrollable giggles that lasted the whole way home.

Chapter Thirty-Four

Maddie slowed outside of their Surbiton house and looked over at Jade. She was well aware the giggling was generated by the intense tension to which they'd both been subjected. As it subsided she caught a glimpse of her daughter's face. Fallen. Full of anxiety.

"It's not finished yet, baby girl. We need to see my cop friend. Are you up to it?"

Jade hiccoughed then nodded. "Yeah, okay. Better go now before I chicken out."

Maddie grabbed her phone from its holder on the dash and asked Jade to look up 'Ethan'. "Ring him. Identify yourself as my daughter and tell him we're on our way with some vital information. No time for anything else or someone will get away with murder."

Maddie listened to Jade speaking to Ethan. He promised he'd be at the kerb in five minutes outside the High Street police station in Kingston.

Which he was. He let himself into the back seat of Maddie's car. "We can talk easier here. What's the rush?"

"I'm about 90% certain Donald Dymock, gym teacher at Horscliffe, raped and murdered little Linsey Benton," she said, twisting so she could talk to him face to face. She didn't mention Geneva's rape. That would come when the moment was right. "And he's about to get on a plane to the United States. Leaving today."

"Okay, give me more. We've interviewed all the teachers at the school, by the way. Nobody was unaccounted for that morning. Why finger Dymock?"

Maddie took a deep breath. "First, I'd like you to meet my daughter, Jade. She was rung by Donald Dymock this morning asking her to come to his house. Something about taking some clothes to his daughter Freya, Jade's great friend, now in New York. Jade knows Dymock both from school and as Freya's father. She didn't hesitate. But he was alone and something happened."

Ethan looked uncomfortable. "Look, there are protocols when there's any hint of impropriety. I can set it up."

"No time, Ethan. Dymock is probably on his way to Heathrow now. Although he might have a headache."

"Mum threw him down the stairs," Jade said with some pride in her voice.

"He threatened to kill me, Ethan. He had me around the throat. Choking me."

"He said he'd throw her head first onto a stone floor a full storey below them," Jade said, emotion clogging her voice. "All because he wanted his stupid phone back. But I figured you'd see when he rang me if I had his phone. Proof. So I nicked it when I found where he'd put the phones, mine and his."

"What?"

"Forget it. Just that I have his phone. It's here." She handed it to Ethan. "Turn it on, please. But first you'll see a text which has come in from British Airways."

He frowned but poked the bottom button. "Okay." He tried to open the phone but it was password protected. "British Airways. I presume it's a courtesy notification for his flight."

"See? We said he was going out of the country. And, by the way, nothing happened to me, okay? Just that he came onto me. I shouldn't have had a swim in their pool when I saw he was swimming too. Except it was hot."

He frowned. "You're not making much sense, young lady."

"I know. Sorry. Tell him, Mum."

"Dymock is a murderer, Ethan." Her voice was calm. Confident.

"Come on, Maddie. Why Dymock?"

"First, do you agree that the person who orally raped Geneva Hopworth also raped and murdered Linsey Benton?"

"Yes. Well, 90% likely. No, probably 98% likely."

Maddie went over her tale, including the bit about a man identified as a Mr Timmig by a hard-of-hearing secretary of the genealogy society. "It looks as if Mr Timmig offered a free ticket overseas to the one person who can corroborate Henry Macgregor's time in the charity shop when buying his fancy clothes for the luncheon with his daughter. An eye witness – looking from afar, I must admit – described him as muscular, tanned and fair haired and appearing as if he was fresh off the veldt."

"So, a semi-deaf person heard 'Timmig' instead of 'Dymock'?" He looked sceptical.

"It's possible. Only probable when you hear the rest of it." Maddie kept her voice even. No good rising to the bait.

"Go on, then."

"So Dymock is a gym teacher who is, what? Muscular, tanned and fair haired and looks like a South African Boer. And Timmig or Dymock made sure a vital witness is now head-down doing genealogical research half the world away. A witness who can exonerate your favoured suspect. Unfortunately, she's a self-proclaimed Luddite about modern technology and essentially out of contact."

"Don't forget Donald knows a lot about genealogy, Mum," Jade said. She turned to look over her seat in front to the policeman seated in the back. "He's into it. He brags that he's descended from one of William the Conqueror's knights."

"So Dymock could have been at the genealogy meeting, is that what you're saying?"

"That's certainly one aspect of it," Maddie said.

"How did he know to go to the genealogy meeting, where, presumably the witness was speaking?"

"He was a member. Look, the meeting took place several days before the murder. The Chair, who is the woman who eventually witnessed the purchase of clothes at the charity shop, spoke about long lost relatives in South Africa. Donald Dymock is quick witted. He saw an opportunity and grabbed it."

"Had Dymock any connection with South Africa?"

Maddie sighed. "No." She tried to keep the frustration out of her voice. "Look, you lot grabbed Henry Macgregor and that suited Dymock mightily. Then there was word of a witness who could corroborate Macgregor's alibi for the time. Dymock just ran with the cards he was dealt and took advantage of the situation. He put two and two together. And the result was within a day or so your star witness was winging her way as far south as it's possible to get."

"Okay," Ethan said. "But how did he hear about the witness?"

"Probably through me, I'm sorry to say," Maddie said. "I talked about finding a witness at the charity shop who can give an alibi for Henry Macgregor. She's a lovely lady but a talkative soul. All who attend the genealogy meetings know she volunteers at the charity shop because she talks about it to all and sundry. Dymock heard her mention South Africa at the genealogy meeting and created the Grand Fantasy."

"Actually, it was all through me." Jade looked again at Ethan. "Probably. I told Freya because Mum found that one of her guys had told the truth about his alibi. And that was interesting and I like it when she figures out that sort of thing. Anyway, Freya's dad could have been there when I told the story. We were in the kitchen. I know Freya's mum was there."

Ethan scratched his head. "I don't know. It's all a mad jumble of semi-connected details."

"If it's a jumble, it's my fault," Maddie said. "Sorry it's coming out so fast. It's just that Dymock is leaving and I'm trying to bring you up to date on way too much, way too fast." She went on to tell him about meeting Geneva and how her story had changed since she was a twelve-year-old. Telling him that Geneva is willing to make a statement describing the darkness of the cleaning cupboard, the stretchy cleaning rag which was pulled over her head and what the rapist said to her. Jade's eyes were fixed on her mother.

"And Dymock often walks to school along the tow path," Jade said. "Or runs."

Ethan turned to her. "Gym teacher who runs, that right?" Just a bit of sarcasm.

Jade nodded. "Whenever he can. He's a fitness freak."

"He works at the school. In fact his office is right by the gym which is right by the changing rooms," Maddie said. She had heard the sarcasm even if Jade had not. "And don't forget Geneva has always claimed no other car was in the carpark but Henry Macgregor's, but that does not mean nobody other than Macgregor was in the school."

"Of course, but…"

"One last thing, Ethan," Maddie said. "I want you to hear what Jade told me earlier." She swivelled to Jade. "Tell him what he said to you when he was pushing you again and again under the water this morning. What did he say to you?"

"Underwater?" Ethan asked. "Look, in the evidential interview, we can go over…."

"Yes, yes. But I want you to hear just this one thing. Something he said to her." She turned to her daughter.

Jade looked at Ethan. "The same thing as Geneva heard when she was …," Jade gulped. "I didn't know that about her until now. Right this minute – I'm hearing it at the same time as you. But I see why Mum's mentioning it, because…. Anyway, when he was pushing me under and sort of groping me, he said, 'Isn't this fun!', all enthusiastic-like. Except I wasn't having fun. Not at all. But it's sort of crazy the rapist used the same words when he was with Geneva."

·· • • • • • • • ··

Maddie and Jade watched Ethan bound up the ramp of the police station shortly thereafter. He had assured them he'd set up the evidentiary interview with a psychologist (a 'lovely' psychologist) as soon as he possibly could. Maybe even tomorrow.

Maddie's shoulders sagged. Nothing was going to happen. Dymock would be away before anything could be done. She didn't start the motor. Instead, she looked over at Jade. "Where to?"

Jade closed her eyes then slowly smiled. "Heathrow."

Maddie smiled back at this amazing daughter of hers. She started the car. "Hoped you'd say that."

Chapter Thirty-Five

M addie headed for the short term carpark. She hated driving around Heathrow. First, because it was always busy with drivers changing lanes unpredictably who also hated driving around Heathrow. But second, because the huge number of signs all had to be read or she'd get hopelessly lost. Instead, she slowed and told Jade to read aloud every sign while she concentrated on finding her way around the many roundabouts, navigating to the correct lanes at traffic lights and avoiding crashing into cars whose drivers were obviously as confused as she was.

Once parked in the appropriate building, they headed inside busy Terminal Three. "You're sure about this?" Maddie asked as they marched over to the British Airways section.

"Of course. And don't remind me again that he might have already gone through security to the gate. But if he has tickets for that 7:50 flight, there's still a chance, Mum. Don't get cold feet now."

"I'm not. But it's up to you. You can change your mind. Leave it to the police."

"As if! Come on. Hurry up," Jade said impatiently. "It doesn't matter if we run. Loads of people do when they're late." She sped up with Maddie attempting to keep up behind.

British airways had queues. Two long ones. The two of them split; Jade went to one and Maddie the other.

Suddenly Jade's voice rang out. "There he is!" She paused. "That man molested me – grab him before he gets away!"

Faces turned her way.

Maddie rushed over as Jade elbowed her way into the crowd of suitcase-dragging people. "There! The guy in the leather jacket!"

Donald shot an irritated look at Jade. Smiled uncertainly to the people around him. Said something.

"That's him! He's a sex abuser!"

As Maddie closed in on him, he blanched, dropped his carry-on bag, turned and ran.

"Stop him!" Maddie yelled.

The customers quietened, watched the drama. Moved to allow the two of them access.

"He's getting away! Call the police!" Her voice soared.

One man stuck his foot out as Donald tried to elbow past him. They both went down with a thud.

"Hold him! Someone, get security!" Maddie yelled.

The man who had tripped Donald up, perhaps not the epitome of fitness but who certainly carried a lot of extra weight, sat on his back.

"Get off me," Donald yelled. "I can hardly breathe."

"Pleased you now know what it feels like," Maddie muttered. She grabbed first one of his hands then the other and got the large man to hold them while she pulled off her silky scarf and used it to bind Donald's hands together.

Donald jerked in an attempt to free himself, first trying to buck the big man off his back, then attempting to kick the man with bent knees. Unsuccessfully. Maddie motioned to Jade to wait until his legs were straight for a moment and they both pounced – Maddie onto his knees and Jade, his ankles.

Maddie turned to the on-lookers, all in various states of dismay. "Scarf, please, someone. I need to tie his feet together."

An elegantly dressed older lady whipped off her matching scarf and handed it to Maddie.

With arms and legs secured, Maddie, Jade and the obese man watched with some equanimity as two burly security men approached.

"Would you please call the police?" Jade asked from her place on Donald's ankles.

"Inform DI Ethan de Roque, Metropolitan Police, Kingston, that you have Donald Dymock in custody here at Heathrow," Maddie said in her most authoritative voice. "He knows all about this creep."

· · · · ● · ● · · · ·

"That was you?" an incredulous Kim asked Jade as they waited for the school to let them in the next morning. "I read about it in the paper. It didn't say who was involved. Just Heathrow, a teenager and one of her teachers."

"Me. And Mum. The man was Mr Dymock. He, like, tried it on with me earlier yesterday. And he was about to skip the country."

"Mr Dymock?" one of the other girls asked. "Sheesh, he tried to get me to do things to him, too. A couple of years ago now, the dirty bugger."

"So he's done it before," Jade said, deciding she'd better keep quiet about Geneva. "We tried to get the police interested. Well, they were interested but they didn't do anything. Red tape."

"I heard a girl last year left school because of something to do with Mr Dymock," someone else said.

"Why have I never heard anything negative about him at all?" Jade asked.

"You were such friends with Freya. Nothing to do with her," the girl who had the incident with Dymock said. "I hate him. Not her. She can't help who her father is."

"I read he was arrested," Kim said.

"So far, not arrested," Jade said. "Just 'helping the police with their inquiries'."

"Well, we all know what that means," Kim said. "He's toast."

· · • • • • • • · ·

Ethan dropped by as Maddie was taking fresh scones from the oven. She had wanted to do something domestic, as far from paedophile teachers and crazy antics at the airport as possible. She was pleased Jade had headed off to school without complaint.

As Ethan ate his way through the fresh scone (with butter and strawberry jam), he told her Jade had been busy.

"She let the cat out of the bag at the school today," he said.

"I'm sorry," Maddie said. "Just too much excitement yesterday, I guess."

"Don't be sorry. I've had two more complaints about Mr Donald Dymock as a result. Important complaints, both young women are having evidentiary interviews this afternoon."

"You'll want Jade's, as well, I suppose."

"Yes. But these two are different. Both had schoolgirl crushes on Dymock. Both described themselves as shy. Each had been hugely complimented that Dymock paid them attention. So they were willing. But one was fourteen and the other fifteen, so, of course, couldn't legally give consent at the time. Both tiny girls, both still look younger than they are. One is seventeen now and the other eighteen."

"He raped them?"

"The Bill Clinton type of rape."

"Oh," Maddie said. "You mean, like Geneva Hopworth."

"Essentially, but not a one-off like hers. Theirs was ongoing."

Maddie winced.

"But, speaking of Geneva Hopworth," Ethan said, "she's come forward with a new statement. It'll be useful." He gestured to the pile of scones and Maddie nodded. "Looks like your boy will get another look from us, too. Officially, at this point, his conviction might be 'unsafe'."

"That's the first good news I've heard," Maddie said. "Please, Ethan, don't let Henry rot in prison any longer."

He sighed. "I wish I could wave a magic wand. But you'll be pleased to know we're recommending his release on parole again. That should happen very shortly. As soon as I get the go-ahead, I'll let you know. Even before his present probation officer." He winked. "But his conviction still stands, Maddie. Nothing as big as that has changed so far. But my team will be busy, very busy, in the coming days. They like cold cases they can solve."

When Jade arrived home, she told her mother about the two other girls who had experienced something similar to her. "Then, as I was walking home, this other girl caught me up. She asked me about what had happened. When I told her, she said hers was way worse."

"Do you know this girl?" Maddie asked.

"Sort of. We were in the school play together last year. She's a year younger than me."

"Did she say how it was worse?"

"She was asked if she'd like to help him after school with putting the equipment away. She was really chuffed at being asked. Thought he was wonnnnderful." She elongated the word. "Then one day he came onto her. She said he wanted her to do stuff – you, know, like Geneva – when he was sitting at his desk. That meant she was underneath the desk where nobody could see her. Sometimes people would even come into the room. He would talk to them. All the while she was under the desk doing it to him. So gross."

Maddie was appalled. "Oh, Jade, I'm sorry she told you all that. Not nice to hear. And scary for you."

Jade shrugged her shoulders. "I know. But we'll see. I think talking about it openly at school is good, you know." She sighed.

"Anyway, she also told me about her breaking it off with him."

Maddie wasn't sure she wanted to hear any more. "Jade...."

"No, listen. This is the one good part. Sort of funny, anyway."

"Okay."

"She'd started playing in a community orchestra a year or so ago. And this guy was sitting next to her. Both play the violin. He goes to Tiffins. Same age as her. They got talking – usual stuff – and she found him interesting. And he found her interesting, too. A couple of geeks, I guess. Really great for her because she's so shy. He did become her boyfriend, but that was later. In fact, he still is her boyfriend."

Maddie nodded. Good to hear some normal stuff.

"Anyway, much earlier, like just after she met this guy, she went into Donald's office and closed the door but stayed there, her back against the door, her hands still on the doorknob so she could run if she needed to. He, the pervert, looked up at her, surprised she wasn't heading to her spot under the desk. She wanted to say it was time for her to find a boyfriend so would not be 'helping him with the equipment' any more. 'Helping with the equipment'! What a jerk."

"She told him she wanted out?"

"She started to say it, but, look, she's shy. Like not self-confident. She sort of stumbled about wanting a boyfriend. He said, would you believe, 'A boyfriend? But you've got a real man.' She then said, 'But I want a real boy!'"

Maddie laughed with Jade, but felt that sinking feeling in the pit of her stomach. Donald Dymock was a pervert, just like Jade said. And the sooner he was out of circulation the better.

Chapter Thirty-Six

Maddie's phone rang.

"Hi, girlfriend. How's it going?" Caroline asked.

"Which bit?"

"Still got a job? Still got a marriage? Those bits."

"Still got the job although I'm not sure if I can stick it anymore, truthfully, Caroline. And still in my marriage and ditto."

"Not good. Tell me if you want a girls' weekend at the cottage in Oxfordshire. Not 'if'. 'When.'"

Once off the phone, Maddie thought long and hard about skipping away again for another restful and soul-renewing break from her troubled life. Soon. But she had some challenges to get through before planning such a thing again.

And leaving Wayne alone for a whole weekend? Not on your life.

· · • • • • • · ·

The opportunity came a day later. Both Maddie and Jade had gone to the police station during the day. Maddie made a statement for the record and Jade had her 'evidentiary interview'.

"How was it?" Maddie asked while she was driving Jade back to school.

"Okay. Not so great remembering it in so much detail," she said. "But the lady was nice. Made it seem okay to be talking with a stranger about something so revolting."

"Good at her job," Maddie said.

After school Jade had gone out to Esher for a study-sleepover with her friend Kim. Thank heavens for Kim, with Freya away and presumably still in the dark about what had occurred between her father and her best friend. Maddie spared a thought for her; life was about to become dreadful for her. Poor Freya. But no Jade meant there was an opportunity for the heart-to-heart Maddie needed to have with her husband.

That evening Maddie deliberately kept to their normal routine. Everything was as Wayne would expect. He arrived home on time. Called out when he arrived. As he always did.

Maddie said, "Hi, Wayne. How was your day?" As always.

He popped his head into the kitchen, said his day had been fine and asked what they were having for dinner.

"Chicken in a Madras curry sauce. Over what's called 'cauliflower rice' instead of real rice."

"Why?" He was already turning towards the living room and its television.

She patted her tummy. "Good for the beer belly."

"Who has a beer belly?"

"Had a look in the mirror lately?" She smiled. Just a tad maliciously.

"Whatever," he said, grabbing the remote.

Dinner was fine. He asked where Jade was, chatted about his music, everything as usual.

When she poured their cups of tea, she sat down and looked at Wayne.

He looked at her, down at his tea, back at her. "What?" Slightly annoyed.

"You," she said and sipped her tea, more so her hands had something to do than she wanted to drink.

"Me, what?"

"You and, well, me, I guess. Or you and whoever you're seeing." She felt her face flush. She grabbed the teacup again, gulped a big mouthful and almost burned her tongue. "Tell me, Wayne. Speak to me."

"What do you mean, 'whoever'? I'm not...."

She interrupted. "Please, Wayne. The truth. Just the truth."

He stared at her. He untangled his right hand from the teacup and placed both palms on the table top. He took a deep breath. "Nothing's happened."

She continued to keep her eyes on his. She knew not to interrupt now he'd started.

"Look, she's got a beautiful voice. It suits our sound. And she's, well, she's attractive. A bit like our Olivia. Actually they used to go to school together."

Maddie dropped her hands into her lap below the table. She gripped them. Tightly. She wanted to erupt. She squeezed her hands even tighter.

A friend of Olivia's?

As young as their daughter?

Attractive?

Instead she loosened her hands, squeezed them again. Hard. Clenched her jaw so she wouldn't make a sound. She continued to stare at him. Took a long, deep breath and held it.

"She knows I'm married," he said. "She's not. Lives with her mum. She's lonely. We know it's wrong. It can't last. She's too beautiful. She'll be off with someone else once she gets her career off and running. That part's mutual – when her career takes off, mine does too. You can see that, can't you Maddie? I'm lucky to have found her."

She didn't deign to answer that one. But she thought she could speak now. Had to speak now.

"The truth, Wayne. Nobody has that sort of discussion before something happens. Only after."

He flushed red again. "You're too smart for your own good," he muttered.

Maddie wanted to scream to the rafters. If they had rafters. Wanted to rush out of the room, slamming the door. Or throw something.

Instead, she sat as if nailed to her chair. "The truth, Wayne. We've always been truthful with each other. It's no time to start lying now."

Tears welled up in his eyes and she could feel her own suppressed tears threatening. "I don't want to hurt you, Maddie. I love you."

She cleared her throat. "I love you, too, Wayne. But I have to know. How long has it been going on?"

"Not long."

She let the silence drag on. She unclenched her hands and sat on them.

"Truly. Just the past couple of weeks. That's all."

Weeks. She cleared her throat. "What do you want to happen?"

"Gawd, Maddie, I don't know!" His voice rose in anguish. "I don't want this to break us up. We have too much together. Years, Maddie. And I know she'll move on. Can't you just forget it? Let it play out?"

She let her breath out slowly. "Play out?" she asked, keeping her voice flat. "No." She shook her head. "No."

The silence dragged on again. She was fighting with herself not to take the blame. Because of her guilt about ignoring him. Of not being interested enough in his music when she knew music was his life – his very being.

At the same time, she also wanted to call him every name in the book. To insult him. To attack this pathetic little schemer who was lonely. Lonely?

Maddie squeezed her eyes shut. How did all this make her feel? Worse than lonely, that's for sure. She shivered at the intensity of her feelings.

Wayne stood and walked around behind her. He lightly massaged her shoulders. "I'm sorry," he said. "Sorry, sorry, sorry. I never wanted to hurt you. But…." He took a deep breath. "But I can't give you an answer right now." His voice choked up. "It'll be soon, Maddie. Soon. I promise."

Chapter Thirty-Seven

Maddie sat a long time at the kitchen table. Wayne was in his usual place, in front of the television set which was turned up louder than usual. Protecting himself from thinking, most likely. She finally got up and saw she'd been sitting there only about ten minutes. It felt like hours.

Once she'd cleaned up the kitchen and made a fresh pot of tea for herself – she certainly wasn't about to offer Wayne another cup – her phone rang.

Jade.

"You got to Kim's all right?" Maddie asked, fearful she'd been diverted from her usual slight worrying, and something had gone wrong.

"Yeah. Kim's mum picked us up. We've had some study time already and a swim in their pool. Pizza for dinner. Everything is fine, Mum. Are you okay? You sound a bit funny."

"Fine, Jade. I'm in the kitchen and your father's watching television. As usual." She was pleased her voice came out naturally, finally.

"Right. Well, I just thought you'd like to know Kim texted Freya. It's early afternoon over there. And Freya rang back."

Maddie's heart thudded. "And?" she asked.

"And Kim told her that her father had come onto me. I wasn't there, Mum. I was in the kitchen helping with the dishes and talking to Mrs. Hogan. Kim had excused herself after dinner. When she came back after, oh, maybe twenty minutes, she told us what had happened. It wasn't me doing anything, honest."

Maddie realised Jade thought her mother would assume she'd orchestrated it. But she knew Jade well enough. Things were so delicate with the police, Dymock and the two of them being so involved with his arrest, Jade would understand she'd have to stay well away from stirring up the pot.

"I know you wouldn't, Jade," Maddie said. "But tell me what happened before I travel down this phone line and shake it out of you!"

Jade laughed her relieved laugh and Maddie relaxed.

"Kim had thought about us not knowing other girls had been targeted by Donald. Nobody at school wanted to tell us. Mostly, nobody wanted to tell Freya about her father. So, Kim decided Freya needed to know everything and right now before someone else told her. Like the police. Or, worse, her mother. Otherwise, she'd be super furious at us."

"There's some wisdom in that, I suppose," Maddie said. "But difficult to do."

"I sure wouldn't want to do it. But Kim's shy but brave, you know?"

Maddie wouldn't call Kim shy. More self-possessed and quiet. Mature for seventeen.

"She told Freya that not only did her father come onto me, but several other girls, too. And for some, way worse. Like, they're all now discussing maybe it was him who'd done it to Geneva then got to like it."

Maddie shivered. Teenaged girls, figuring things out for themselves. But not talking to any adults about it because the subject was taboo.

And whose fault was that?

"Poor Freya," Maddie said. "It must have been very difficult for her."

"When Kim told me, I texted Freya saying if she wanted to talk, to just ring."

"Has she?"

"No. But she'll have to sort things out inside her head, I bet. Before she rings." Her voice dropped. "Or decides not to ring."

"And we have to respect that, "Maddie said in an equally soft voice. "You okay?"

"Yes. Fine. But all we can talk about is bloody Donald."

"Does Mrs Hogan know?"

"Yeah. We told her. She's horrified, of course. But not going crazy about it. She's okay."

"Try to get some studying in, Jade. That's why you're there."

"Will do."

After saying she'd see Jade when she got home tomorrow after school, Maddie went upstairs. She had no desire to bring Wayne up to date on the latest.

· · · ● · ● ● · · · ·

The next morning, she dithered about informing Ethan. But he rang before she could decide.

"I've just had a telephone call I know you'll be interested in," Ethan said.

"Go on," she said. Interesting enough to ring? She was listening with all ears. "Who from?"

"The principal of Horscliffe. Suddenly, he's all informative."

"Like he wasn't before?"

"Like he definitely wasn't before." He drew a long breath. "Seems our Mr Gym Teacher was the subject of a parental complaint a wee while ago. Inappropriate suggestions to a schoolgirl."

"And the principal hadn't said anything about it when you questioned him after Linsey's murder?" Maddie was aghast.

"He says he put it down to a schoolgirl's fantasy. But I have a feeling this wasn't the first."

"Come on, Ethan. Why?"

"Because he put Dymock on notice – extra supervision, that sort of thing. More importantly, gave him some friendly advice to start looking for a new position, meaning 'resign or I fire you' in anybody's language. It doesn't fit. If this was the first complaint and the principal dismissed it as an adolescent crush, why threaten the guy's job? So not the first complaint. Covering his arse. But the most interesting part of all is the date. Tell me, Maddie. When did this happen?"

"No," she breathed. "Really? Damn him to hell. Actually, both of them."

"Yes," he said, no teasing in his voice at all now. "Indulge me, Maddie. When?"

"The day Linsey Benton was killed. Of course." Dymock's lifestyle threatened. More than threatened. Finished. At least in this country. "He would have been spiralling out of control. Bottled up fury. Ready to explode."

"And took it out on a young schoolgirl," he said. "I knew you'd put it together. We're a good team, Madeleine Brooks. Don't you dare quit your job."

"Yes, well…"

He barked a laugh. "There's more. I must thank your daughter, too."

"About which part of this increasingly involved story?" Maddie raised her eyebrows even though Ethan couldn't see her.

"The part about nicking Dymock's phone."

"You found the call he made to her?"

"Yes, that. But something a bit more important. And an explanation about why his response to her nicking his phone was so over the top."

"Come on, Ethan. Spill."

"He'd taken photos through some sort of peephole into the girls' changing rooms at the gym. Some were still on his phone."

"The sleazebag!" OTT? Certainly was, and then some. Threatening to kill her by throwing her over the bannister? More than a sleazebag. Beneath contempt. A monster.

"And he likes the little girls. The eleven and twelve-year-olds. Most of the photos were of pre-pubescent kids." He sighed. "Also, I think your daughter has been busy again," he said.

"The international phone call?"

"Calls," he said.

"Not Jade this time. One of her friends, though." She paused. "Did you say 'calls', plural?"

"I did. Donald Dymock received a call from Freya. His daughter in New York."

"Did he now...."

"Apparently someone called his daughter. Gave her the dirt about her father and her friends. She called him. And I can tell you, he came off that call in a bad state. He then rang his lawyer who dutifully came in. Dymock wanted to make a new statement."

"You're drawing this out, Ethan," Maddie said.

He chuckled. "Guilty. And so is that pervert. We've got the bastard, Maddie. He admitted it all. Every last bit including selling those kiddie pics on the dark web. And he confessed to the rape of Geneva Hopworth all those years ago."

"Really?"

"Really. He was distraught by the daughter's phone call. And his lawyer's advice was that it was all coming out, so getting it all done and dusted early would act in his favour."

"He'll get life?"

"Possibly. Probably. The only question will be how long the non-parole period will be."

Maddie came off the phone and felt a relieved grin spread across her face. A confession. Jade wouldn't have to testify. Henry would get his conviction quashed. Geneva wouldn't have to relive it all in front of the world.

Sometimes, good things happen.

Chapter Thirty-Eight

Maddie had agreed to go back to work. Against Caroline's advice and Jade's too. But Wayne, as expected, was all for it. She had agonised over her decision and had no illusions about how Romania would treat her. But with the Wayne situation being so delicate, Maddie had to be practical. One major problem at a time, and first in the queue was family. She had to stabilise things for Jade who had been too involved for any student in the midst of exams. And who didn't need any major changes in her life.

And Maddie had to discover whether or not she still had a marriage in spite of Wayne's avowal to break it off with the 'lonely' singer. As a consequence, Maddie was due to start back at the Probation Service on Monday. Thank heavens she had today for Henry.

She arrived first. It was a gracious room with views out over the Thames featuring rowers practising for some race or other, slow moving riverboats with potted gardens on their roofs and motorboats buzzing in the sparkling sunshine. London at its best.

She had chosen quite deliberately to have a formal afternoon tea to celebrate Henry's release from prison. It was primarily a treat for a friend. But also a chance for Henry to wear his good gear again out in public, the gear purchased in his favourite charity shop that fateful day.

When she spotted him, he looked every inch the gentleman that he really was. And had always been.

He walked over to their table and sat down. "Maddie, my dear, you look lovely."

She stifled her honest response that she'd had this dress forever and said, simply, "Thank you, my friend. It's not often we have a chance to dress up."

"Weddings, funerals and afternoon teas," he said with a smile.

"Nice shoes," she said. "Have I seen them before?"

"Yes. That day I was thrown back in prison," he said. "Suitable for this outfit; suitable for my luncheon with my daughter and now afternoon tea with you. Old shoes but my shoes tend to last forever. All good shoes do. My one vanity; I always used to spend decent money on my footwear – you've noticed my Ecco casual shoes before – and they, and these shoes as well, date from long before I was arrested all those years ago."

"Which type did you wear to school?" Maddie kept her voice casual.

"These ones. Nothing like footsteps in the schoolroom to focus attention onto the work the pupils were supposed to be doing. Slowly approaching footsteps, an unspoken sign of authority, if you will. Always jacket and tie. My working uniform."

With Dymock's confession Maddie knew it, but she still felt relieved at the confirmation of her assumptions about his shoes.

The waitress brought a silver tower of tiny sandwiches and placed it on their table. Another waitress came with a teapot and cups and saucers on a trolley, complete with sugar cubes, miniscule tongs and milk in a white porcelain jug matching their teacups.

"Have you heard from DI de Roche?" Maddie asked as she put several of the savoury sandwiches onto her plate.

"Yesterday. He's promised to do all he can. Now Kathy is back and has made her statement about my buying the clothes that critical morning, he's all smiles. Did you know she picked Dymock out of a line-up as the 'South African' Milhousen who financed her trip?"

"Did she now," Maddie said. "So the gift of the plane ticket really was all about getting her away. To give Dymock time enough to remove himself from England, I suppose. I wonder if he really did have that job in the fancy school in New York."

"As a confirmed paedophile, I bet he does. Or, if not there, somewhere else with young girls." He sipped his tea in its delicate cup. "I learned quite a bit about paedophiles while away. I was unfortunately included in their select little group. And we needed to band together. My fellow cons were hard on paedophiles. We were the lowest of the low."

Maddie didn't reply, just lifted her cup in a silent salute to what he'd been through.

"My case is now officially an application for a 'miscarriage of justice' and it's been referred to the Criminal Cases Review Commission."

"Good," Maddie said. "So Dymock's confession is holding water. Thank goodness he confessed to the rape as well as the murder."

"All due to those teenaged girls. I particularly would like us to acknowledge young Geneva Hopworth. What a brave young woman. It takes a lot to admit you misled the police. And was responsible for my incarceration. The wrong man sent to prison. But it makes sense: she was a frightened twelve-year-old child and I was the only man she saw."

Maddie heard the tone of his voice. Not a scrap of anger or vindictiveness. "I have to warn you that the Commission takes ages, Henry. They are quite overwhelmed with cases, I gather. But they should refer you to the Appeal Court in the end, all going well. And, by that time, Dymock's trial and sentencing will be well over. It should be okay."

"And, during all of it, I'm not in prison." He said it in a heartfelt way. "I don't mind being on parole for however long it takes. Although I wish it could be with you, Maddie." He paused. "But we are friends and we can sneak off for the occasional cup of coffee, perhaps."

She nodded and raised her teacup.

"To friendship," she said.

The End

Also by Tannis Laidlaw

Death in Cold Waters is the first in the Madeleine Brooks
Mystery series. The others, all stand-alone meaning the series
can be read in any order, are:
Book 2:

Death at Cherry Tree Manor

Book 3:

Death at Valley View Cottage

Book 4:

Death in Lachmore Wood

Book 5:

Death at the Olde Woodley Grange

E-book stand-alone psychological suspense novels:

Bye Baby Bunting (also in paperback)

The Pumpkin Eater's Wife

Half Truths and Whole Lies

Thursday's Child

Marcia's Dead (to be released 2022)